## "You'd be okay if Striker whispered

"Sure," Erin replied. *Yes. Anything. Just don't stop.*

He eased the straps of her dress down over her shoulders. "Stay on your stomach."

She nodded.

As he inched her dress lower, the neckline rasped over her nipples and she sucked in a quick breath.

"Okay?" he asked.

"Fine," she replied.

Her skin had turned supersensitive, and she had a crystal-clear vision of Striker's rough hands on her breasts.

He went back to the sore spot between her shoulder blades, then gradually worked his way down her spine. His fingertips were strong and sure. Her muscles couldn't decide whether to relax in ecstasy or tighten in arousal.

Erin didn't know what heaven felt like, but she was sure it had to be close to this.

Dear Reader,

I'm thrilled to be publishing the second book in the Reeves-DuCarter brothers' series. This time it's pilot Striker Reeves-DuCarter the maverick of the family, who meets his match in a jewelry buyer from New York City.

Over the past few years I've been fascinated by the discovery, development and marketing of diamonds in Canada's far north. When emeralds were discovered as well, I knew I had to use the northern gemstone industry in a story.

I hope you enjoy another glimpse of Tyler and Jenna Reeves-DuCarter, from my earlier Harlequin Temptation novel *Next to Nothing!* And I hope you enjoy reading Striker and Erin's story as much as I enjoyed writing it. I'd love to hear from you at www.barbaradunlop.com.

Best wishes,

*Barbara Dunlop*

## Books by Barbara Dunlop

**HARLEQUIN TEMPTATION**
848—FOREVER JAKE
901—NEXT TO NOTHING!
940—TOO CLOSE TO CALL

**HARLEQUIN FLIPSIDE**
22—OUT OF ORDER

**HARLEQUIN DUETS**
54—THE MOUNTIE STEALS A WIFE
90—A GROOM IN HER STOCKING
98—THE WISH-LIST WIFE

# BARBARA DUNLOP

## FLYING HIGH

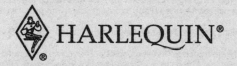

HARLEQUIN®

TORONTO • NEW YORK • LONDON
AMSTERDAM • PARIS • SYDNEY • HAMBURG
STOCKHOLM • ATHENS • TOKYO • MILAN • MADRID
PRAGUE • WARSAW • BUDAPEST • AUCKLAND

If you purchased this book without a cover you should be aware
that this book is stolen property. It was reported as "unsold and
destroyed" to the publisher, and neither the author nor the
publisher has received any payment for this "stripped book."

To Mom with love.
You make so many things possible
for so many people.

ISBN 0-373-69206-4

FLYING HIGH

Copyright © 2005 by Barbara Dunlop.

All rights reserved. Except for use in any review, the reproduction or
utilization of this work in whole or in part in any form by any electronic,
mechanical or other means, now known or hereafter invented, including
xerography, photocopying and recording, or in any information storage
or retrieval system, is forbidden without the written permission of the
publisher, Harlequin Enterprises Limited, 225 Duncan Mill Road,
Don Mills, Ontario, Canada M3B 3K9.

All characters in this book have no existence outside the imagination of
the author and have no relation whatsoever to anyone bearing the same
name or names. They are not even distantly inspired by any individual
known or unknown to the author, and all incidents are pure invention.

This edition published by arrangement with Harlequin Books S.A.

® and TM are trademarks of the publisher. Trademarks indicated with
® are registered in the United States Patent and Trademark Office, the
Canadian Trade Marks Office and in other countries.

www.eHarlequin.com

**Printed in U.S.A.**

# 1

IF STRIKER REEVES had the slightest interest in a lecture and a stern reprimand, he would have said *yes* to the gorgeous black-haired, leather-skirted fireball who'd approached his table last night at Carnaby's on Leicester Square.

But he didn't.

And he hadn't.

And he was getting way too old for this.

His father, Jackson Reeves-DuCarter, leaned forward, voice tight as he placed his broad hands on the back of the tufted leather chair. "And then I hear that five, *five* of my top executives were forced to twiddle their thumbs in Paris because of you."

Striker felt a muscle tick in his left cheek. It was only his mother's presence in the dining room next door that kept him from walking out of his father's office, quitting his job as a jet pilot with Reeves-DuCarter International on the spot and leaving his parents' house.

Instead, he counted to three, forcing himself to keep his voice low. "If you'll recall, *I* was the one who stuck to the schedule."

Jackson's dark eyes glittered. "The schedule is subject to change. That's why we have our own jet. That's why we don't fly commercial carriers."

"Then maybe you should hire a whole team of pilots, so one of us can be suited up, at the ready twenty-four-seven."

Jackson shifted in front of the expansive bookcase, where his deep-seated opinions were reinforced by business administration textbooks penned in the fifties. "Not much point in having a pilot suited up when *you* take off with the jet."

Striker counted to three again. His father might be willing to devote every waking second to the betterment of the family corporation, but Striker wasn't a corporate robot. He was a flesh and blood man.

"I'm entitled to a life," he said.

Jackson scoffed. "Is that what you call it? A life? I call it a joyride. And I'm getting sick and tired of you using my airplane to pick up women."

Striker bristled. "It was a *date*, not a pickup, and the jet belongs to the corporation, not to you."

"Then next time, take your ten percent to London and leave my sixty on the tarmac where it belongs."

Striker's mouth curved up in a smirk. "If you want to get technical, I only used it ten percent of the time."

Jackson obviously didn't appreciate the joke. His voice turned calculating. "If you want to get *technical*... When can your mother and I expect to meet your new *girlfriend*?"

Striker shifted. Jeanette definitely wasn't coming to Seattle anytime soon. He wasn't even sure he remembered her last name.

He'd met her in a Paris nightclub. Like many women, she'd been impressed by the fact that he was a jet pilot. When she'd asked for a ride, he'd figured what the hell? Take her on a quick hop over the Channel and see where things went from there.

Unfortunately, by the time they got back, he'd maxed out on hours. So, when the executive group wanted to leave Paris early, Striker couldn't fly.

"Just as I thought," said Jackson with a shake of his head. He pulled out the desk chair and sat back down, picking up a gold pen. "You're out of control, Striker."

"Because I have a life?"

"Have a life on your days off. When you're on the job, you're on the job."

Once again, Striker started to silently count.

Jackson didn't even let him get to two. "I'm grounding you for a month."

It took a second for the words to sink in. Striker took a step back. "You're *what?*"

"I've hired another pilot."

"That's ridiculous." And it was humiliating, and totally uncalled for. Striker was a grown man, not some errant grade-school boy. "You want me to write lines on the chalkboard, too?"

"It had crossed my mind."

"I'm thirty-two years old—"

"Some days, I find that very hard to believe."

"You can't do this."

"I just did."

Striker took a sharp breath. He opened his mouth, then snapped it shut again. His father was the CEO of Reeves-DuCarter International, and Striker was nothing but an employee and a minor shareholder. Arguing would get him exactly nowhere.

But there was *one* thing he could do. Something he should have done a long time ago.

Without another word, he pivoted on his heel and headed for the door. He'd have his letter of resignation typed up within the hour.

Ground him? Striker didn't think so. His father might be the all-powerful CEO, be he was hardly the FAA. There were millions of other aircraft out there, millions of jobs for which Striker was fully qualified.

He strode determinedly into the dining room, where his mother was setting silverware out on the glass-topped table. In the center, a oriental vase was filled with white roses and artistically twisted cherry blossom branches. The place settings were her best royal blue china.

He slowed his pace to say goodbye, deciding to tell her about quitting later. No point in upsetting her right before dinner. Plus, he honestly wasn't sure if he could blurt it out to her face.

She turned from the table and patted his arm.

"Striker, honey, can you run down to the wine cellar for me?"

He paused, making sure he kept his voice gentle. "I'm sorry, Mom, but I'm not going to be—"

"Tyler and Jenna are finally coming for dinner," she said, "and we need a second bottle of merlot."

Striker put a little more determination in his voice. "Mom, Dad and I just had another—"

She tipped her head sideways and hit him with an impatient look. "Now, Striker, you know there's no point in talking to your father at this time of day. Go get me the merlot. You haven't seen your brother in ages."

The expression on her face and the rush of words told him she knew something was going on.

Had she overheard their argument? Had Jackson confided his "punishment" to her? She had to know that Striker would never stand for it.

"Jacques is making salmon in dill sauce tonight," she continued, turning back to the table. "You know it's your favorite."

Salmon in dill sauce might have placated Striker when he was twelve, but he was past the point of being bribed by Jacques. He sighed. "Mom."

"For dessert we're having white chocolate mousse."

He leaned sideways over the table in an effort to catch her eye. "Mom, I really am going—"

"Don't be silly." She made a shooing motion with

her hands, refusing to meet his eyes. "Be a good son and go get the wine."

Striker hesitated, frustration warring with loyalty, sharp words about his father hovering on the tip of his tongue. After a moment's hesitation, he swallowed them. How the hell was he supposed to quit his job when he couldn't even cut out on a family dinner?

Quitting would kill his mother.

He knew that.

He'd always known that.

She'd worried for years while his brother, Tyler, worked at his own business. And she'd been over the moon when her youngest son had finally come back to work at Reeves-DuCarter International last month, and the family was together once again.

If Striker left now, he'd pull the rug out from under his mother's newfound happiness. What kind of a man would do that?

ERIN O'CONNELL couldn't believe her boss would *do* this to her. "*This* is what you call my big break?"

"I'm asking you to schmooze with him, not sleep with him," said Patrick Aster in an undertone, closing the boardroom door on the busy reception area of Elle Jewelers' New York head office.

"For *schmoozing,* the company's buying me a new wardrobe?" Erin felt like a prostitute. Sure, she'd been bugging Patrick for months to give her a chance to negotiate with some of their bigger gem suppliers, but not like this, not at the expense of her ethics.

Patrick walked over to the coffee station and poured himself a cup. "This is Allan Baldwin we're talking about," he said. "Allan *freaking*, High Ice Diamonds, Baldwin. Do you have any idea what kind of an opportunity I'm handing you?"

Erin crossed her arms over her cream colored blouse. "Exactly *how* will flirting my way into a contract get me recognition and *respect* in this company?"

Patrick lifted the stoneware mug as he turned to face her again. "You land the Baldwin account, and this company will kiss your little white—"

"They'll all think I slept with him to get it."

Patrick scoffed. "No they won't."

"Yes, they will."

He took a sip of the coffee. "Well, even if they do, they won't care."

"You don't get me at all, do you?"

A smile played on his lips and his eyes danced. "You're intelligent, committed, hardworking and hungry."

Okay. So, maybe he did get her. She'd been a regional buyer for Elle Jewelers for four years now and she was dying to break out into the big leagues. But she had her standards, and she had her pride. She wasn't about to use her gender, her looks and her body to get her first big gemstone contract.

Patrick sighed with exaggerated patience. "All you have to do is fly to Seattle, hop a floatplane to Blue Earth Island, attend the Pelican Cove Art Exhibition—I wrangled you an invitation—and 'accidentally' run into Allan Baldwin."

"Then offer him *what* to sign with us?"

Patrick winked. "Whatever it takes, baby."

Erin's jaw dropped open.

"I'm joking, Erin. It's done like this all the time. You meet him casually, get to know him, put him at ease before you start talking business."

"No."

The boardroom door opened and Elle Jewelers gemologist, Julie Green, stuck her head in.

Patrick nodded in her direction. "You can take Julie with you."

"Take Julie with you where?" asked Julie, coming fully into the room and closing the door behind her.

"To Seattle," said Patrick. "The Mendenhal Resort on Blue Earth Island. All expenses paid."

"The Mendenhal?" asked Julie, her blue eyes going wide.

"Elle Jewelers will throw in a new Fuchini wardrobe," said Patrick. "For each of you."

Julie turned to Erin, her short blond hair bobbing with her rapid nods. "Yes. Take Julie with you. Definitely."

"Don't get so excited," said Erin. "He's pimping us."

Julie looked back at Patrick for a second, then back

to Erin. She mouthed the word *Fuchini.* Then out loud she said, "Define pimping."

Erin rolled her eyes.

"Have you *seen* their summer dress line?" Julie shot Patrick another look. "I wouldn't actually have to sleep with anybody, would I?"

"Allan Baldwin," said Erin.

"*The* Allan Baldwin?" asked Julie.

Erin wasn't surprised that Julie recognized the name. Allan Baldwin had revolutionized the diamond industry.

With his huge diamond find in northern Canada, he'd capitalized on the demand for ethical stones. When he "branded" his diamonds by etching a microscopic killer whale into each stone mined at his High Ice property, the market had leaped to attention. Now every jewelry wholesaler in the world wanted Allan's gems. Including Elle Jewelers.

"*The* Allan Baldwin," Patrick confirmed.

Julie's eyes narrowed and her mouth puckered contemplatively. "Well… He *is* gorgeous. I mean if I had to actually sleep with—"

"Gorgeous is all it takes for you to throw your principles out the window?" asked Erin.

"Of course not," said Julie, much to Erin's relief. "Drop-dead gorgeous and a diamond mine is all it takes."

Patrick chuckled.

Erin shook her head.

"Didn't you see his picture in *Entrepreneur West* last month?" asked Julie.

Erin had seen the picture. Allan was definitely good-looking.

Not that his looks made any difference. Patrick's proposal was ridiculous. She threw up her hands. "I'm a professional gem buyer, not a good-time-girl."

"Men do this all the time," said Patrick. "Tell her, Jules."

"Men do this all the time," said Julie.

"What men?" Erin challenged.

Julie looked to Patrick.

"Jason Wolensky," said Patrick.

Erin paused. Jason Wolensky was one of Elle's top international buyers.

"And Charles Timothy," said Patrick. "They both had a shot at Allan Baldwin, but they blew it."

Julie nudged Erin. "I told you those millions of hours on the butt master would pay off one day."

"So, I'm getting a chance to best the who's who of Elle Jewelers buying staff because of my glutes?"

Erin wasn't ready to accept that. Growing up in a stuffy little apartment in the Bronx, she may not have had much, but she'd had her mother's wisdom. Her mother had always told her that with hard work and perseverance a person could accomplish whatever they wanted. She'd never said anything about having good glutes.

Patrick took a step forward. "Erin. Jason tried.

Charles tried. Believe me, they used everything they had. If Allan was gay, they would have used their glutes."

"Allan's not gay," said Julie with an air of authority.

"I'm not asking you to step over any ethical boundaries," said Patrick. "Fly out west and meet him. Talk to him. Laugh with him. Then offer him our best terms and see if he says yes."

Erin hesitated. Despite Patrick's smooth sales pitch, this didn't sit right with her.

"I can guarantee you a promotion to senior buyer," said Patrick.

Okay. That seriously sweetened the pot. Maybe her ethics *could* be bought for the right price.

"There's an empty office on the ninth floor," Patrick continued.

Erin felt her resolve weaken. She definitely wouldn't offer sex… Maybe she wouldn't even have to flirt… Schmoozing wasn't flirting…

She could buy a dress that thoroughly covered her butt…

"You're a professional," said Patrick. "Now get out there and give it your best shot."

Julie linked her arm with Erin's. "And take Julie with you."

STRIKER CUT the oil drain-plug lock-wire on the engine of his Cessna floatplane and positioned the drain pan beneath. He was sweaty, dirty and tired, but his father's words still cycled relentlessly through his brain.

Then he'd hear his mother's soft voice, see the vulnerable look in her eyes, and he'd know that he had to find a way to make things work with his father—no matter what. He had no idea how he was going to do that, but walking out wasn't an option.

In an effort to focus on something, *anything* besides the sorry mess that was his professional life, he'd spent most of the day combing a local airplane boneyard for parts for his three planes. Banging his way through decommissioned aircraft seemed like one of the more productive outlets for his frustration. He might not be able to quit his job and still live with himself, but he sure as hell didn't have to stay on the ground.

His Tiger Moth and his Thunderjet were stored in a hangar at Sea Tac. They needed months, maybe years worth of work before he could take them up. But the Cessna floatplane was definitely airworthy. Maybe later on this week, after he'd sweated out some more of his anger, he'd take the little Cessna up for a spin.

A freshening wind moved in off the Pacific, sloshing rhythmic waves against the barnacle pillars of the Seattle floatplane dock. He moved the engine cowling out of the way and crouched beneath the plane to break the oil drain-plug loose with a wrench.

"Excuse me?" a female voice came from the other side of the plane.

Fingertips working the stiff plug, Striker glanced in the direction of the voice.

He could see legs, gorgeous legs, strappy little high-heeled sandals and the hem of a short skirt.

Under normal circumstances, he'd be more than interested in those legs and that voice, not to mention the second pair of legs hovering just behind the first. But these weren't normal circumstances.

He gave the drain-plug a final crank and it dropped into his hands. He quickly pulled back as the oil whooshed out, splattering into the pan below.

He straightened, coming around the propeller, wiping his hands on a rag.

The women's bodies and faces definitely did justice to their legs. The closest one reminded him of a lady he'd met in Australia. She had shoulder-length, sandy-blond hair, mysterious brown eyes and a hint of freckles beneath her carefully applied makeup.

She was wearing a stiff white skirt with a zipper up the front. Her gauzy mauve blouse told him she had both confidence and style. She was pretty and pouty—the kind of woman whom life had probably dealt few blows. Though at the moment, she was obviously frustrated.

The other woman looked amused. Striker liked that.

Her short, wispy, sunshine-blond hair lifted in the breeze. Her eyes were blue, and her makeup dark and sultry over a copper tan.

Striker turned his attention back to the pouty one.

Challenging as she looked, he didn't have the time
nor the inclination to try to coax her out of her mood.

"Can I help you with something?" he asked her.

She trapped her windblown hair and pushed it
back over her shoulders. "The office was locked."

"The office?"

She tilted her head toward the small Beluga Charters building at the top of the wooden ramp. "We had
a plane booked for five o'clock."

"It's six-thirty," said Striker.

"Are you our pilot?"

"I'm *a* pilot. But not yours."

Her hand went to her hip and she locked one leg.

Oh, yeah. This was definitely one woman who always got exactly what she wanted.

"Our flight from New York was delayed," she
said. "But we still have to get to Blue Earth Island."

"You should probably call Beluga in the morning," Striker suggested.

"We need to get there tonight."

"Can't help you." He had parts to strip, airplanes
to build and frustration to work out of his system.
Gorgeous as she was, this woman did not look like the
type to offer a no-strings-attached frustration outlet.

Not that sex would help solve his problem.

"Why not?" she asked. "You're here. Our real pilot
left. We did call and leave a message on the machine
as soon as we hit Sea Tac. I can't imagine anyone
would object if you took care of the customers."

Striker had to admire her tenacity and straight-ahead logic. Didn't change his mind. But he had to admire it.

"You're not *my* customers," he pointed out as the engine oil continued to splatter noisily into the pan behind him.

She moved a little closer.

Oh, great, here it came.

Female coercion on his six.

"I'm sure you'd get brownie points from your boss for helping out," she said. "Above and beyond the call of duty and all that."

"You've obviously never met my boss," Striker drawled. Flying beautiful women around for Beluga Charters or anyone else would definitely not earn brownie points with Jackson Reeves-DuCarter this week.

"It wasn't our fault we were late," she said.

"Never suggested it was. But I don't work for Beluga Charters."

The metallic echo of the oil drip behind him trickled to nothing.

"Who do you work for?" she asked.

"Today? Myself."

"Great. We'll pay you to fly us to Blue Earth Island. Cash."

Striker jerked his thumb back toward the engine. "I'm changing the oil."

"How long will that take?"

"I'm not flying anybody anywhere."

She captured his gaze with liquid brown eyes and a long, slow blink. "How much?" she asked softly, getting under his skin for a split second.

Striker stuffed the oily rag into the back pocket of his jeans. "More than you've got."

"Try me."

"Listen, you're a beautiful woman—"

Her brown eyes darkened. "What does that have to do with anything?"

"I'm sure you're used to guys falling all over—"

"I'm not *used* to anything. My plans fell through. I need to charter a plane. And I'm willing to pay you whatever it takes to get me to Blue Earth Island by seven."

"I'm not for sale, and I have at least an hour's worth of work left on my engine."

She took a breath, which pressed her pert breasts against the thin blouse.

Yeah.

She never used her looks for anything.

Right.

"How soon can you get us to the island?"

"I'm not getting you to the island."

"If you were. How soon?"

Striker knew he shouldn't answer that question. He knew he was being manipulated by someone who'd had practice. But her eyes were warm. Her lips were soft. She was stunningly beautiful. And, despite her protests, that *did* count. "An hour and a half."

"That's too long."

"Good thing I'm not taking you."

She pursed her pouty lips, glancing around the deserted dock. "Is there somewhere we can change?"

That threw Striker. "What for?"

"If you're not getting us to the island until eight, we need to dress for the reception before we go."

Striker had had enough. He didn't have time for a difficult woman, and he sure wasn't explaining his position one more time.

"The hell with this," he muttered, swiping his sweaty hair from his forehead with the back of his hand. He held the drain-plug up to the light to check the gasket.

"Well, the hell with this," the woman echoed under her breath.

The gasket looked fine, so Striker crouched back under the engine and wiped the oil drain with his rag.

She crouched down and unzipped her large suitcase.

Curious, despite his resolve, he watched her out of the corner of his eyes.

To his amazement, she pulled out a black dress and yanked it over her head. Then she proceeded to writhe her way out of the blouse beneath. A man would have to be made of stone not to get interested.

"You got a mirror in your purse?" she asked her friend.

"Sure do." The friend followed suit, opening her suitcase and pulling out her own black dress.

Striker glanced around the dock, checking to make sure he was their only audience. "Uh, ladies…"

"Erin O'Connell," said the pouty one. "And this is Julie Green."

"Striker Reeves," said Striker out of ingrained habit.

Erin whipped a lacy white bra out from under the dress, settling the clingy fabric against her mouth-watering curves. Then she shimmied out of the skirt beneath. "We'll give you a thousand dollars to fly us to Blue Earth Island."

Striker shook his head in self-disgust. He was *so* easy.

# 2

ERIN GLANCED AT her watch and then squinted at the chain of islands in the distance. "Can't you fly a little faster?"

"This is a floatplane, not a fighter jet," said the man named Striker.

The little plane bumped again in the turbulence, bringing her up hard against the shoulder harness in the right front seat. The stiff strap bit into her bare shoulder, and she was sure the lap clasp was wrinkling her dress. "You said eight o'clock."

Striker slowed the plane down, yet again. "I *said* I wasn't taking you. And I shouldn't have taken you. I'm going to have a hell of a time landing in this chop."

"What time do you think we'll get there?"

He glanced at her and smirked. "I'm not about to give you anything to hold me to."

"I'm only asking for an estimate." She figured nine at the outside to even make the last few minutes of the art reception. If they weren't on the island by nine, they had a very big problem.

He shook his head. "No guess."

"Eight-thirty?" she asked.

"It's eight-fifteen now."

"Nine?"

"Maybe."

Julie leaned forward, holding a magazine between the two front seats, speaking loudly over the drone of the radial engine. "Here's the latest article on him. That man is the catch of the century."

"Nine at the very latest," said Erin to Striker.

"You still have to get from the dock to town," he pointed out.

Her heart sank. "How long will that take?"

He shrugged.

She fought an urge to swear at him. "Five minutes? An hour? You must be able to give me a range."

"By the time you call a taxi? Probably forty-five minutes."

She closed her eyes and slumped back in her seat. They were toast.

"They estimate his wealth at eight figures," said Julie, dropping the glossy magazine into Erin's lap.

Erin half-heartedly glanced down at the open page. Fat lot of good the information would do her now.

STRIKER SHIFTED his gaze from the horizon to the magazine in Erin's lap. There was too much vibration to read the headline, but he wondered whose net worth they were talking about.

Eight figures? Catch of the century? They sounded

Barbara Dunlop 25

like a couple of husband hunters. Maybe they were rushing to the island because Prince Charming was going to turn into a pumpkin at midnight.

He realized it was a jaded reaction, but he'd met a lot of women over the years who saw his bank account and his jet plane a whole lot more clearly than they saw him. And Blue Earth Island was an exclusive little resort area. Erin and Julie wouldn't be the first to try reeling in one of the seasonal residents.

"It says he's expanding the emerald exploration work this year," said Julie, leaning forward in her seat.

"We're not going to make the art reception," said Erin.

"We'll meet him some other way," said Julie.

"How? Hang around town like a couple of stalkers?"

"Don't be such a defeatist. The man's got emeralds."

"Maybe."

Julie pointed to a spot in the magazine print. "They're already drilling portals. If the mineralized zones pan out, he could be sitting on a second fortune. For that, we stalk."

"You are shameless," said Erin.

Striker turned his attention back to flying. Mineralized zones? Portals? If these women were looking for rich husbands, they'd sure done their homework.

"Absolutely," said Julie. "If they're gem quality, I'm his for life."

Striker snorted to himself. And here all these

years, he'd thought a jet plane was a good strategy for picking up...well, *dating* women. Apparently diamond and emerald mines worked even better.

Erin flipped the magazine back to the first page of the article and Striker recognized the man in the picture.

"That's Allan Baldwin," he said, surprised they were talking about someone he knew. Not that he hadn't heard about Allan's diamond find. Everybody in Seattle knew about the local man who was on his way to becoming a billionaire.

Striker peered at the picture for a moment. From the same upscale Seattle neighborhood, he and Allan had known each other most of their lives. Though Striker didn't see him often anymore. The last time was at a university fund-raiser over Christmas.

Striker took in the perfect haircut, the salon tan and the three-thousand-dollar suit. "He used to dress a lot more casually."

Erin's brow creased. "You know him?"

Striker shrugged. "Sure."

She paused for a second, peering at Striker, her expression turning puzzled. Then she held up the magazine, index finger tapping on Allan's face. "You know this man?"

"Uh-huh."

Her gaze traveled slowly from Striker's worn work boots to his stained jeans to his torn T-shirt.

Her obvious disdain made him feel like a bug under a microscope.

Talk about a snap judgment. Just because he was dirty and oily and sweaty didn't mean he was some lower life-form. He'd put in a hard day's work today. Something little miss impractical shoes ought to try sometime instead of focusing on landing a rich husband.

"You know Allan Baldwin?" she asked one more time.

"Am I not speaking English? We went to high school together."

A light dawned behind her eyes and she turned her attention back to the magazine with a nod. "Oh. High school."

Now that was vaguely insulting. Like he couldn't possibly know Allan in adult life. Apparently he was good enough to ferry the women across the sound, but he'd best keep to his station in life.

Wouldn't she be shocked down to her pretty little shoes if she got a look at his stock portfolio.

Not that he was going to enlighten her. No way did he want to get on her husband hit list. If they found out his ten percent of Reeves-DuCarter International put him in the eight-figure range right along with Allan, he might as well paint a bull's-eye in the middle of his chest.

Julie leaned forward from the back seat, excitement coloring her tone. "You know, Erin...he might be able to help us out."

Erin stilled, eyeing Striker up and down again, a disconcertingly calculating expression on her face. This time he felt like a side of prime beef in a butcher's window.

"Are you thinking what I'm thinking?" asked Julie, the pitch of her voice going up.

"Exactly how well did you know Allan Baldwin?" asked Erin.

Striker couldn't believe where they were heading, looking down their noses at him one minute, using him as a go-between the next. "Give me a—"

"We can clean him up a little," said Julie, with obvious excitement. "Give him a shave. Buy him some decent clothes."

Striker felt his irritation building. Clean him *up?* Like he couldn't be a suave, debonair guy when he felt like it? He'd never had so much as a single complaint about his personal hygiene. And, at his mother's insistence, he owned at least half a dozen, custom-made tuxes.

These women would be mortified to know who they were talking about cleaning up.

Erin turned those powerful, bedroom-brown eyes on him. "You don't have to get right back to Seattle, do you?"

Oh, sure. She was the woman who never used her looks for *anything*. She could write a book on how to change a man's mind with eyelashes alone. But he wasn't about to take time out of his life to help them snare Allan.

"This may shock and surprise you," he said. "But even *I* have a life."

"We can pay you," she countered.

Could she insult him any more thoroughly in the space of five minutes? "Money is not an issue."

Erin took in his dirty clothes again. "You were quick enough to take the thousand."

Striker clamped his jaw shut before he said something he'd regret. Like admitting it was her sexy eyes and not the thousand that got him in the cockpit.

"We'll put you on the payroll," she offered.

The *payroll?* Just how organized were husband hunters these days?

"And we'll buy you some new clothes," Julie chimed in. She glanced down at her black dress. "We got Fuchini, but I think you're more of a Valnadi."

Striker hated Valnadi.

Erin's brows knit together. "You think you'd be able to make contact with Allan Baldwin after all these years? I mean, without making him suspicious?"

"Read my lips," said Striker. "I am not helping you get to Allan."

Erin turned back to Julie. "You know, Allan might think Striker's after his money."

"Excuse me?" Allan wasn't going to think Striker was after his money.

"That's why we have to fix him up," said Julie.

"It'll be a big job," said Erin.

"*Excuse* me," Striker said a bit louder.

They both stopped talking and looked at him.

"I *am* sitting right here in the plane."

Julie grinned. "Sorry."

He shook his head in disgust. "What part of *no* do you people not understand?"

Erin's expression faltered for a second. Then she seemed to regroup. She took a deep breath and put a hand lightly on Striker's shoulder. "I know you're probably nervous. But, I promise, it won't be that difficult."

"Damn right it won't be that difficult," he said. "It'll be the easiest thing in the world."

She smiled, and his pulse reacted.

He cursed himself for being so susceptible. "Because all I'm doing is dropping you off and flying back to Seattle."

Her smile died. "You can't do that."

"Watch me."

"Are you intimidated by his success?" Her husky voice sizzled the length of his spine, making him think of dark nights and long, slow lovemaking.

He was sure she'd planned it that way.

"You don't have to be intimidated," she said. "We can help you make a good impression. What to say. When to say it. Which fork to use."

*Etiquette* lessons? Striker had dined at a five-star

Paris restaurant just last Thursday, and nobody'd complained. He hardened his tone. "I'm not the least bit intimidated by his success."

A broad smile broke out on her face and those liquid brown eyes glowed with approval, sending sparks coursing through his body. "Good," she said, giving his shoulder a little squeeze, making him wonder if she lived her entire life in denial.

"I believe I said no," he pointed out, ignoring the reaction of his skin to her soft fingertips.

"Why would you do that?"

"I have things to do." Not that he needed a reason.

"I'm sure they'll wait."

"You don't even know what they are."

The warmth of her palm made its way through his T-shirt sleeve, playing havoc with his resolve as she leaned a little closer, her voice dropping. "I don't think you understand. This is really important to us."

There she was, up close and personal, using every trick in the book, making him want things he couldn't have, changing the chemistry of his blood.

"I thought you said you never used your looks for anything?"

She blinked, drawing back. "Who's using looks? I'm trying to reason with you."

Like hell. "You're flirting." And it was seriously working.

"I'm schmoozing. There's a difference."

"You're touching me."

"I'm touching your *shoulder.* If I was flirting, I'd touch your chest, or maybe your neck or maybe your hair."

She might as well have touched him in all those places. Her words sent a straight shot to his groin.

"I'm making a business proposition," she said.

"And I'm saying no."

"Then I'm offering you more money."

"I'm still saying no."

"Then I'm appealing to your better nature."

"I don't have a better nature."

"We have a spare bedroom in our beach house. Right on the water. View of the sunset."

Striker's mind didn't make it past "bedroom" and "our beach house." He'd always been a sucker for promises women couldn't keep. No wonder he was forever taking them on joyrides.

"Fine. I'll give you twenty-four hours."

"Forty-eight," she said.

"No way."

ERIN COULDN'T believe she'd resorting to *schmoozing* before they'd even made it to the island. Sure, they needed Striker's help—desperately now that they'd missed the art reception. But she'd practically fawned over the man's shoulder.

And she hadn't even realized she was capable of that please-sleep-with-me tone of voice. Patrick dangled a promotion in front of her eyes and she instantly turned into a shameless flirt.

It was undignified. And she wasn't going to do it again. Not that she'd have to. Now that she had Striker on board, things would run a lot more smoothly.

As soon as the taxi came to a stop, Julie jumped out of the front seat. "Will you *look* at that ocean?"

The setting sun had turned the entire world pink, and white-water crescents reflected on the waves as they roared on shore fifty feet away.

Julie kicked off her shoes and sprinted onto the sand.

Without a word, Striker began lifting the suitcases out of the trunk. He'd stayed peevishly silent for most of the taxi trip, and Erin knew he was annoyed. But he was the one who'd agreed to help them. Nobody had held a gun to his head.

They'd stopped at the Mendenhal Resort's office on the way through the gates to register and pick up the key. Now Erin unlocked the door and stepped back to let Striker carry the load of suitcases inside.

"Where do you want the gigolo?" he asked, setting down the suitcases and gazing to where the rough hewn, wood-railinged staircase ran the length of one wall, up to a second floor balcony. Three doors opened off the balcony into rooms at the back of the house.

"You are *not* a gigolo," Erin insisted, even as the word conjured up a totally unwelcome image of the big, rangy Striker.

She shook it off. He was nowhere near her type. And he was only here to introduce them to Allan. There were *no* other duties involved.

Striker carried in the second set of suitcases. "You're paying the rent and buying me clothes."

"There's a perfectly good reason for that."

"Yeah. I'm a kept man."

"Get over it."

"Easy for you to say."

She rolled her eyes.

"Okay," he said. "What would *you* call me?"

"You're a consultant," she said.

Striker gave her a mocking grin. "That sounds *so* much more dignified."

"Doesn't it though?"

"Okay. Well, just to make sure your *consultant* understands the plan of attack…which one of you is trying to land Allan?"

"I am," she said.

"Why does that not surprise me?"

"Well, I'm the project lead. Julie's here for technical advice."

At least that was the excuse Patrick had come up with for sending Julie on the trip. Truth was, there weren't any diamonds for Julie to look at. And even if there were, it wasn't necessary. High Ice Diamonds reputation for quality was well established.

Striker's eyebrows went up. "*Technical* advice."

"That's right." Erin glanced around the high-ceilinged living room of the West Coast log house. "Not that I'm going to need it."

It was a beautiful building and a beautiful setting, right on the beach in the classy little town of Pelican Cove. There were skylights in the two-story living room ceiling and a massive stone fireplace against one wall. If a woman was going to kiss her principles good bye, this was as good a place to do it as any.

Striker leaned against one of the log walls, crossing his arms on his chest and resting one ankle over the other as he contemplated her. "I have to say, you're pretty open about your plans."

Erin blinked at him. "You did ask. And you are on the payroll now. We're not going to tell Allan everything right away, of course. That's why we hired you."

"Of course," said Striker. "Him knowing what's going on, that might put a cramp in your style."

"It wouldn't make things any easier. That's for sure." She picked up one of the suitcases. Might as well get settled. The sooner they got started on Striker, the sooner they could arrange a meeting with Allan.

Striker took two long strides toward her. "Wouldn't want you to get calluses." He reached for the suitcase, lifting it easily with a broad, strong hand.

"What?" she asked.

"Detracts from the diamonds," he said, picking up a second suitcase and heading for the wide staircase.

Erin stared at his back for a minute. She was going to buy the diamonds, not wear the diamonds.

"Or maybe you'd prefer a few emeralds," he called over his shoulder.

Erin started up the stairs. "Quite frankly, I'd like to get my hands on both."

"A truly mercenary woman."

"I'm a professional."

"I don't doubt that in the least." There was an edge of sarcasm to his voice.

Maybe it was a mistake to bring a man like Striker in on this, no matter how valuable he'd be in meeting Allan. "Does it bother you that I'm after his diamonds?"

"It's not like you're the first to try."

"Really?" Erin reached the top of the stair and drew alongside him in the twilight hallway.

That surprised her. Had other gem buyers come to Blue Earth Island to approach Allan? Had Striker flown them over? Maybe there was more to this than an old high school acquaintance.

If he *had* flown the other buyers in, maybe he had some valuable information about them. Maybe she could get him to spill it. Not that she was going to schmooze with him again. But there had to be a professional way to ask.

"Of course you're not the first," said Striker.

The three upstairs bedrooms had en suite plumbing and queen-sized beds. The middle one was slightly smaller, and the two on either end had balconies.

"I'll take the middle," he said. "Since I'm the help."

He headed to the far end of the hall with Erin's suitcases.

She stood in the doorway while he dropped the cases on the bed, trying to come up with a way to broach the subject of the people on his previous flights.

"Striker?"

He turned to look at her. "Yeah?"

The stark assessment in his ocean blue eyes made her stumble. Focus, she told herself. Ask him. *What were the other buyers' approaches? How did Allan react? What mistakes had they made?*

No. Those were too blunt.

"Spit it out," he drawled, cocking his head to one side.

"I was just..." She tried to formulate subtler questions.

He took a step closer, his deep voice thrumming in the silent house. "Whatever it is, you're going to ask eventually. Why wait?" He shrugged one of his shoulders forward and his tone turned teasing. "Unless you want to touch me again first. You know, schmooze me."

"*No.*" She shrank back. "I don't want to touch you."

His eyes sparkled at her sharp reaction and a dimple appeared in one of his cheeks. She suddenly realized that beneath the dust and dirt, he was a incredibly attractive man. Not that she cared. Not that his looks were relevant.

"You want to flirt with me again, Erin?"

Her name on his lips gave her a little shiver, but she shook it away.

"I never flirted with you the first time."

"That's your story, and you're stickin' to it?"

She took a deep breath. "You mentioned there were…other people who tried to get Allan to sign a contract. Do you know how they—"

"A *contract*?" The dimple disappeared.

"Yes."

"Is *that* what you call it?"

"What would you call it?"

He shook his head and let out hollow chuckle. "Whatever."

"What?" What had she done now?

"Maybe it's none of my business. After all, I did agree to help. But don't you think calling it a contract is a little mercenary?"

Mercenary? "It *is* a contract. A diamond contract."

Striker snorted and shook his head. "And here I thought I'd heard it all."

"Hey, it's done like this all the time. There's nothing illegal or immoral about schmoozing."

"Ahh," said Striker. "Schmoozing again. We both know how much you like *schmoozing*."

His tone irked, but she refused to let herself rise to the bait.

"Schmoozing is only the window dressing," she said. "And it's not like we'll keep him in the dark until the last minute." She was vaguely aware that her defensiveness made her sound guilty, so she put some more strength into her tone. "He'll have a chance to consider the whole deal on its merits."

Striker's blue eyes narrowed. "You don't find this all just a little too...calculating?"

"I consider it a prudent, professional approach." Or at least Patrick did, and since Patrick was her boss, and since she desperately wanted that promotion, this was the approach she was taking.

Striker rolled his eyes.

"What? How would *you* suggest I go about it?" If Striker had a better idea, she was all ears.

He moved a little closer, increasing the impact of his stare. "What about ditching all the clandestine plotting? Meeting someone legitimately? Letting them get to know you? Maybe falling in *love?*"

Erin felt as if the floor had shifted beneath her. She gave her head a little shake. "In love?"

"Yeah. You know. The old-fashioned way."

His words made no sense. "You're suggesting I try to get clients to fall in love with me before signing a contract?"

"Clients? No offense, Erin, but calling them clients makes you sound like a hooker."

Erin opened her mouth, but nothing came out. She tried again and managed a squeak. "A *what?*"

"You're marrying a man for his money."

"I'm not marrying anybody."

"Excuse me. My mistake. You're signing a 'diamond contract.'"

Erin stopped.

She squinted.

She sifted through the conversation.

"Uh, Striker?"

"What?"

"What is it you think I'm doing here?"

He raked a hand through his shaggy hair. "Trying to get Allan Baldwin to marry you."

Erin let her chin drop down to her chest. She covered her eyes with her palm and shook her head. "Oh, boy."

"What?" Striker sounded puzzled.

She peeked up at him. "I'm trying to get Allan to *sell* me diamonds, not *give* me diamonds."

Striker's brow creased. "Sell them to you how?"

An astounded smile tried to force its way from between her lips. "I'm a wholesale buyer for Elle Jewelers. You may have heard that Allan Baldwin owns a diamond mine."

Striker blinked once. "You're a diamond buyer?"

She nodded.

He blinked again. "Oh, well… In that case… I guess my estimation of your character just went up a notch."

"Why, thank you."

"Don't mention it."

"So, what exactly *is* one notch up from a hooker?"

# 3

AT ASHER'S ON MAIN STREET, in downtown Pelican Cove, Striker watched Erin's dubious expression as he shrugged into an olive-green, double-breasted jacket above a pair of navy slacks. Awash in embossed gold buttons, with lapels out of the seventies, the jacket was tight across the shoulders and loose in the body.

It served her right.

Even if she wasn't trying to land a rich husband, she was still planning to pull one over on Allan. Striker figured he owed it to his friend to at least make her work for the introduction. Besides, it was a kick to feed into her prejudices by playing the uncouth bohemian.

She wanted him so badly? Well, now she had him. And he was going to enjoy every second playing Eliza Doolittle to her Henry Higgins.

He struck a pose in front of the three-sided, full-length mirror, hoping he wasn't overacting. "Now *this* is what I call an outfit."

The salesman stared, his jaw dropping open in abject horror while Erin let out an ill-disguised gasp. Striker could see the panic building on her face.

She was going to kill him if she ever found out he was yanking her chain.

"Would the gentleman like to try the Hillsboro, as well?" the salesman asked diplomatically, holding up a charcoal suit. "Just as a comparison."

"Does it come in brown?" asked Striker.

The man's forehead wrinkled. "I'm...afraid not, sir."

"The gray is nice," said Erin, regaining her composure. "You should really try it on."

Striker made a show of frowning. Truth was, Hillsboro was one of his favorite designers. Though his mother always made a fuss if he bought suits off the rack.

"The burgundy tie would go well," said the salesman.

Striker accepted the clothes. "You sure you don't like this one?" He posed in front of the mirror one more time.

"Not quite right," said the salesman.

"Definitely no," said Erin.

"Okay," said Striker, closing the changing room door behind him and smirking into the mirror inside. This was the ugliest jacket he'd ever seen.

He stripped off the suit and changed into the Hillsboro, which fit just fine. He absently tied the burgundy striped tie while slipping into a pair of loafers the salesman had provided.

He supposed it was time to let Erin off the hook on the clothing front. But he couldn't wait to present her with his medieval table manners, and he had plans to work his way through his entire repertoire of tasteless jokes.

He stepped out of the changing room and spread his arms wide, executing a turn.

She stepped forward and a wide grin broke out on her lips. "That's it!"

Striker ignored her grin, and the resultant warm glow working its way up his legs, leaving a tingling yearning in the pit of his stomach. He was cursed with a Pavlovian response to beautiful women. But there was no time like the present to beat it.

"You sure?" he asked her, pretending to hesitate over the suit. "I think it would look better in brown."

The salesman brushed the shoulder and straightened the back of the jacket. "Very good, sir."

Striker wiggled his shoulders, holding out for just a few seconds longer. "It feels a little—"

"Not at all," said the salesman.

"We'll take it," said Erin.

Striker turned and grinned at her. "How do you get four suits for a dollar?"

Both Erin and the salesman looked at him blankly.

"Buy a deck of cards."

Erin blinked in astonishment.

"Very good, sir," said the salesman.

Striker chortled obnoxiously at his own humor. "I'm going to need some blue jeans, too."

"I'm afraid we don't carry blue jeans," said the salesman.

"We'll definitely take the suit," said Erin. "And an extra shirt, the shoes and the paisley tie."

"Where can we get blue jeans?" asked Striker.

"I believe the Garment Barn on Second Avenue carries western wear."

"What about some pleated chinos?" asked Erin.

"Perfect for daywear," said the salesman.

"Do you have a pair in green?" asked Erin.

As the salesman crossed the store, Striker turned to Erin. "I'd rather have sweats than chinos."

"Trust me. I'm the image expert."

"What's wrong with sweats? They'll make me look like a jock."

"They'll make you look like a couch potato."

Striker leaned in a little closer. "I have abs of steel." He pulled the dress shirt out of his slacks, revealing his bare stomach. "Want to feel?"

Erin's eyes widened in shock. "Will you *stop*."

"Stop what?"

"Stop acting like…like…"

"I'll make you a deal," he said, leaving the tails of his shirt hanging out, trying valiantly not to laugh at her mortified expression.

"Not if it involves me feeling your abs, you won't."

"You want to feel my abs?"

"No!"

"I'll let you think about that one. Offer's open." He pulled the tails of his shirt apart, giving her a come-hither look.

"No."

He shrugged. "Your loss. Okay, let's talk deal over clothes."

"You are *not* getting sweats."

"Deal is, I'll wear whatever you want, whenever you want."

"Finally," she said. "You're coming to your senses."

"In return." Striker paused for full effect, waggling his eyebrows and trying to look as lecherous as possible. "I get to pick an outfit for you."

There was a split second silence while his words penetrated. "No."

Short, sharp, definite.

Striker shrugged. "That's the deal. Take it or leave it."

She lowered her voice, glancing at the salesman across the store. "You can't make deals. You're on my payroll."

"Not if I quit."

She stared at him, looking genuinely worried. "You wouldn't."

This was *way* too much fun. "One outfit. My choice. You wear it."

She bit her lower lip, and he knew he had her.

"Don't worry." He patted her shoulder. "I won't make you wear it in public." Then he moved his mouth closer to her ear. "You can wear it just for me."

She sucked in a breath.

He let his gaze drop down to run the length of her figure. "You do wax?"

She sputtered something indecipherable and he wondered if he'd pushed her too far.

Then he decided he might as well go for broke. "You'll look drop-dead gorgeous in high-cut red and black satin."

Her voice turned to a hiss. "I'm not about to—"

"No more skin than a bathing suit," he promised, offering a Boy Scout salute.

The salesman returned with the slacks, placing them in Erin's arms.

She glanced down at the slacks, then she squared her shoulders. "I think we'll need a Bjorn sweater to go with them."

"Of course," said the salesman.

"I'm going to take that as a yes," said Striker on a note of triumph.

AFTER A LONG and hopelessly frustrating day of shopping with Striker the classless wonder, Erin welcomed the peace and quiet of her bedroom. She opened the balcony door, sighing in relief as the Pacific breeze buffeted the gauzy white curtains, whirling fresh ocean air through the room. Then she flipped open her cell phone and dialed Patrick's office number.

There was a three-hour time zone difference, making it seven in the evening New York time. But she knew he'd still be there.

She could hear Striker in his bedroom next door, unpacking the clothes they'd bought earlier. She couldn't believe any human being could have such singularly bad taste.

She also couldn't believe Striker had thought she was planning to marry Allan for his money. That was nothing short of insulting.

And then he came up with that stupid clothing deal. Like she'd, in a million years, ever wear something sexy for *him*.

She'd refused to even enter the lingerie store, terrified of what feather and starched-lace concoction he might insist she try on then and there. Instead, she'd headed across the street to a café to drink a well-earned cup of coffee.

She'd assured herself there was little risk in letting him pick something on his own, since she was going to postpone wearing it until she found a way out of the deal anyway.

Still, a glance at the discretely wrapped gray package at the foot of her bed sent a distinct shiver of unease through her body. And the thought of parading in front of him wearing next to nothing washed her body in heat.

While the tone of Patrick's telephone echoed in her ear, she opened the glass door wider, shaking off the unnerving sensation.

She wasn't attracted to Striker. Not one little bit.

So, okay, he did have a certain high-testosterone edge that might interest a lot of women.

But not Erin. She couldn't get past his bad taste and his horrible jokes.

*What did the necktie say to the hat?*

*You go on a head. I'll hang around for a while.*

Erin shuddered.

She shoved the gray bag under the bed.

The mere thought of modeling lingerie for him made her skin prickle—and not in a good way. She needed more air. Cradling the phone on her shoulder, she wiggled her way out of the short sleeved sweater she'd worn shopping.

The telephone clicked. "Aster here."

She turned so the wind could caress her back. Ah. That was better. "It's Erin."

"Hey, Erin," said Patrick. "How was the reception? You ready to sign him up?"

She lifted her hair, letting the wind cool her neck. "Well… The good news is, we're on the island."

"Of course you're on the island."

"It wasn't as easy as it sounds."

Patrick paused. "There's bad news?"

"We missed the art reception."

"Damn."

"I know."

"That was your perfect chance."

"Plane was late." She let go of her hair, unzipping her skirt, kicking off her sandals.

Striker banged something in the room next door and Erin had a vision of his brash, uncoordinated movements. They were going to have to work on his walk as well. Bull in a china shop had nothing on him.

"So, what's plan B?" asked Patrick, sounding a little tense.

"We've made contact with a...friend of Allan's." Friend was definitely a stretch.

"That's great." Patrick's tone perked up. "Will you see Baldwin soon? Not to rush you, Erin, but Charles is making noises about trying again."

She paused midshimmy, her tight skirt halfway down her legs. "What do you mean trying again? Charles knows *I'm* on it now, right?"

"Well...not exactly."

"What?"

"I thought it would be better if we surprised upper management with a signed, sealed and delivered contract."

Erin stilled. "Tell me that was a joke."

"I have every confidence in you, Erin."

"Patrick."

"Gotta go."

"Patrick!"

There was a click on the line.

Erin kicked off her skirt and flopped backwards onto the bed. Closing her eyes, she lay her forearm across them. Patrick was risking both of their jobs on this?

She was out here on a high-dollar, high-risk buying trip without the approval of the board?

She had *better* come home with that contract.

There was a knock at the door.

"Erin?" It was Julie's voice.

"Come on in," Erin called, wondering if she should share the turn of events with Julie. Maybe not. Julie's job was hardly at risk. She was little more than an innocent bystander.

The door rustled opened. Erin moved her arm, opened her eyes and turned toward the silence.

Striker stood next to Julie, staring wide-eyed at Erin while Julie smirked.

Adrenaline hit Erin's bloodstream and she let out a little shriek, jumping up from the bed and reflexively folding her arms over her chest. As soon as she was on her feet, she realized she'd made the problem even worse.

They now had an even better view of her scantily clad body, and it was obvious neither of them were about to turn away and save her dignity.

Of course, Julie had seen her in her underwear many times. But Striker could at least close his eyes, instead of staring openly. The man wasn't just low class, he was no class.

She glanced frantically around the room for something to cover herself. Spotting a fuzzy white robe on the bathroom door, she sprinted for it and stuffed her arms in the sleeves, yanking the belt tight around her waist.

"Can I *help* you?" she asked, shooting them both a disgusted look.

"You've already done plenty to perk up my day," Striker drawled. "Thanks."

For a second she thought he was going to actually wink at her.

She groped for the gray lingerie store package and tossed it at him. "We're done now."

He tossed it right back on the bed. "I don't think so. Though, this does confirm that I made the right choice."

Erin glanced at the gray package with rising trepidation.

Julie chuckled. "Lookin' good, Erin. The butt master is paying off big time."

Erin felt her face heat, realizing that while she'd run for the robe, Striker had had an unobstructed view of the panty-clad butt under discussion.

She told herself he was nothing but a low-class charter pilot. Why should she care one little bit about the opinion of a man who liked avocado-green dinner jackets?

Even if he did stare at her as though she were lunch. Even if the heat in his gaze made her feel like she *was* lunch.

His opinion was nothing. He was nothing.

Besides, Julie was right. Erin's butt was doing just fine, thank you very much. And her purple high-cut panties and matching bra were nothing to be ashamed of either.

She squared her shoulders and re-tightened the sash on her robe, through being embarrassed by the likes of Striker. "Tell me what you want."

"We're here to strategize," said Julie, heading into the room and taking a seat on the bed. She planted her elbows behind her, leaning back.

Striker followed but, thankfully, took one of the armchairs near the balcony door. He slouched down, spreading his legs, making himself right at home.

"Striker showed me those great clothes," said Julie, nodding to the chinos and Bjorn sweater Striker had changed into. "He looks like a million bucks. I think we're pretty much ready to rock and roll."

Erin sat down in the other armchair, ignoring Striker's casual pose while she pulled the ends of the white robe primly over her knees. They were no-where near ready to rock and roll.

"We still have a lot of work to do," she said, shooting Striker a sidelong look. "He's not nearly ready."

Striker met her gaze. "What's more to learn? You planning to teach me how to talk with an English accent or somethin'?"

"I want to teach you *not* to be crude and sarcastic and *not* to walk like a professional wrestler. For example."

"You've watched a lot of professional wrestling have you?"

"None."

"Well I have."

"Why does that not surprise me?"

"They don't walk anything like me."

Erin gestured at him with one hand, holding the robe secure at her knees with the other. "You strut. You saunter. You walk into a room like you're about to plant a flag."

"I think that's kind of sexy," said Julie.

Erin shot her a *you're not helping* glare. "I somehow doubt Allan Baldwin is going to respond to Striker being sexy."

"You think I'm sexy?"

"I didn't say that."

"You hinted."

"That wasn't a hint. Can we focus on our strategy?"

"That's why we're here," said Striker. "How about I call him up, tell him I'm on the island with a couple of friends and that we'd like to drop by?"

"Bad idea," said Erin.

"Why? It's simple. It's realistic. It's almost the truth."

"He'll think you're after something."

Striker shifted in the chair. "Getting away for a moment from the fact that I *am* after something, why would he think that?"

"Come on. He strikes it rich. Then, suddenly, out

of the blue, you show up on his doorstep. He'll definitely be suspicious. And if he's suspicious of you, he's suspicious of us."

Striker shook his head. "Allan's not the suspicious kind."

"You know this from…high school?"

Striker didn't answer.

"We have to make him believe you have nothing to gain from renewing your acquaintance. We have to make him believe you're successful, that you have money."

"Why would he assume I wasn't?" asked Striker.

"No offense, Striker, but I can tell you don't have money just by looking at you."

His eyebrows went up. "You can?"

"Sure."

"Just by my looks?"

She eyed his new outfit. Okay, so he looked pretty credible in those clothes. As long as he kept his mouth shut. But that was all her doing.

"It's not just your clothes we have to worry about," she said. "It's your hair. The way you sit, the way you talk. Everything about you gives you away."

Striker gave her a long, unfathomable look. "Really?"

"Yes. Really."

"You're saying Allan will take one look at me and think I'm after his money."

"Exactly."

"No offense, Erin, but you're the one after his money."

"I'm trying to make a business deal."

Striker looked skeptical.

"A business deal that will be beneficial to *both* of us."

"Think Allan will believe that?"

"I hope so."

"I still think I should just call him up."

"Not yet."

"You have to fix me first?"

"That's right."

Striker leaned back and spread his arms wide. "Okay, babe. In that case, I'm all yours. Bend me, mold me, shape me." He paused, letting his gaze caress her for a second. "But I have to say, I think it'll work better if you take off the robe."

Julie laughed.

Erin tightened her sash.

# 4

Mr. Stephen Reeves-DuCarter, representative of Reeves-DuCarter International, would never have stared openly at a woman caught in her underwear. But floatplane pilot and all-around tacky guy Striker sure would. Who could have guessed that being low class would be this much fun?

As he watched Erin on the other side of the kitchen, he played with fond memories of her purple underwear from last night. She might be sharp-tongued and judgmental, but her body was hell on wheels.

Whatever a butt master was, Striker was all for them.

"I'll try to get you an appointment for ten," she said, picking up the telephone, all business. She'd been that way all morning.

They'd finished breakfast dishes a few minutes ago, and Julie had immediately headed for the beach.

"I don't need somebody named *Philippe* cutting my hair," said Striker. "I just buzz it once in a while, then let it grow out until it gets in the way."

He was lying through his teeth. He'd never had a

buzz cut in his life. His mother had been dragging him to upscale clothing stores and hair salons since he was five years old, extolling the virtues of making a good impression.

Erin gave an exaggerated little shudder as she dialed the number. "We are not *buzzing* anybody's hair."

For a split second there, she actually reminded him of his mother.

"Hi," Erin said into the receiver. "I'd like to book an appointment for a haircut." She paused. "This morning, if possible."

"You don't?"

She glanced at Striker, her teeth scraping over her bottom lip. "Thursday? But…"

"Right. I understand. Thank you."

She hung up the phone.

"We buzz?" asked Striker, sitting up straight, picturing his mother's face when she saw him, knowing it would be worth it for the look on Erin's in the meantime.

"No. We do *not* buzz. Take off your sweater."

"Yes, ma'am." Striker jumped up and reached over his head to grab the back of the sweater. "I figure it's a million to one shot you're going to get it on with me on the kitchen table. But, I'm gonna take it." He stripped the sweater off over his head.

"I am *not* going to *get it on* with you on the kitchen table."

"See, I figured that."

"I'm going to cut your hair myself."

"You really are desperate, aren't you?"

She moved to the sink and turned on the water, running her fingertips beneath it. "It's not like I can make it any worse."

"Thanks a ton." His hair wasn't that bad. Sure, it had been a few weeks since he'd had a trim, but longer styles were making a comeback.

"I worked my way through college as a hairdresser," she said, shaking the excess droplets off her hands. "Come over here and soak your head while I find some scissors."

Worked her way through college as a hairdresser? Striker felt a sudden unexpected twinge of guilt. He'd gone through college on the trust fund plan.

Fortunately, the guilt didn't last long. Erin was too tough to need anyone's pity. Besides, the unnecessary emotion was quickly superceded by the thought of her hands caressing his scalp.

Ever since he'd seen her in her underwear, he'd found his thoughts wandering into increasingly dangerous territory.

"A nice woman would wash it *for* me," he said.

"I'm not that nice."

Striker grinned. She was cute when she was defiant. It made him want to kiss her.

Of course, kissing her was out of the question—not that he wouldn't love to see what she'd say after he planted a wide wet one on those pouty lips.

His gaze dropped to her mouth.

Nope. He really couldn't. That would be going way too far.

But he could keep her arguing. That was fun, too.

"How am I going to start thinking like a rich man if you give me a bargain basement haircut? I'm afraid I'm going to need full service."

"Nice try."

"Seriously." He tapped a finger against his chin and pretended to contemplate. "I think this is like method acting. I have to immerse myself in richness for a few hours, get a feel for the wealthy lifestyle. You bring any shampoo?"

Her gorgeous coffee eyes flashed at him. "I am *not* washing your hair."

Striker leaned back against the counter and folded his arms across his chest. "Then you're not cutting my hair."

Erin shut off the taps. "Don't get obstinate on me. You can't go to meet Allan looking like a refugee from Haight-Ashbury."

"Me obstinate? *Me?*"

"Yes."

"Let's think this through a minute. I'm letting you dress me. I'm letting you change my walk, my talk and my personal hygiene. I'm even letting you at my hair. And all I'm asking in return is for one little wash? Who's the obstinate one here?"

Erin opened her mouth.

Then she closed it again. She cocked her head sideways and her eyes narrowed.

Striker waited.

After an obvious mental battle, she sighed. "Fine. I'll get my shampoo."

As she walked out the door, he nearly staggered back in surprise.

He'd won? Hot damn.

A few minutes later, Erin came back into the kitchen with a bottle of fruit extract shampoo and a small pair of scissors.

Striker pulled a chair up to the sink and slouched down, wondering if she would try to get revenge on his scalp. He braced himself.

She turned on the taps and readjusted the water temperature.

"Lean back," she instructed, her palm cradling his head, guiding him over the edge of the sink.

She used the spray nozzle to soak his hair. Then she applied the shampoo and worked the lather in with her fingertips.

To his surprise, her hands were gentle, oddly comforting. After a few minutes, he relaxed his guard, closing his eyes. It seemed harmless enough to enjoy her touch. Heck, it was probably the only chance he'd ever get.

The smell of lime filled the air around him.

"So you were a hairdresser?"

"I was."

"Was it fun?"

"Most of the time."

"What did you like about it?"

"Meeting people. Getting to know them."

He opened his eyes and waggled his eyebrows. "Got to know them well did you?"

She smirked. "Hairdressers and bartenders. You'd be amazed."

"People confessed things to you?"

"Of course."

"Yeah? Anything good?"

She concentrated on his temples, drawing little circles at his hairline. "Sex, scandal, stock market tips. You know. The usual."

"Tell me the sex part."

"Sorry. Sworn to secrecy. It's in the code."

"Come on. You're retired."

"Doesn't matter."

"You can change the names to protect the innocent." She paused.

"They'll never know," he said.

"Well, okay." She grinned. "You want the really racy stuff?"

"Of course."

"You're bad."

"I know it."

"In my junior year, there was this one woman. I'll call her *Thelma*."

"Thelma."

"Right. Thelma carried on a rip-roaring affair with the pool boy. I got intimate details for months."

"Intimate ones?" asked Striker.

"You bet. He was a very good-looking pool boy." Erin's voice hummed softly in his brain. "But it all ended one day when she told me she had to change her hair color. Her husband had refused to let her keep it red."

He opened his eyes again. "You're making this up, aren't you?"

Erin shook her head. "It's all true. Well, except for her name. Her husband blamed the affair on her red hair. Told her it had to be either brown or black from then on."

Erin's voice was soft and musical when she wasn't sparring with him. "I think it was my fault they got divorced."

"How so?"

Her hands migrated to the top of his head. Her movements were slow and deliberate, and Striker's body started to react to the sensuality of her touch. "A few months later, we snuck in some auburn highlights."

"You shameless hairdresser."

She nodded "Right after that, she had another affair. I always thought her husband was nuts, but maybe he was right."

"Oh, yeah. I'm sure it was the highlights."

Her magic fingers moved to the back of his head,

down to the base of his skull, pressing, rubbing, massaging. He never wanted this to end. "You never know."

"Ever think of dying your hair red?" he asked.

"Any interest in a cold rinse?"

Striker chuckled. "You've got a mean streak there, woman."

"That's what happens when you try to flirt with me."

"I wasn't flirting. I was schmoozing."

"Right."

"Hey, I'm not touching a single body part. You on the other hand—"

"Wash is over." She cranked on the taps.

"You're heartless."

"That's right. So don't mess with me." She quickly rinsed his hair, then toweled it off and draped the towel around his shoulders, picking up her scissors.

"You sure you know what you're doing?" he asked.

"Trust me." She moved up close. "I'll have you fixed up in no time."

"Please don't say the word 'fixed' while you're approaching me with sharp instruments."

She obviously fought a grin. "That is another perfect example of the kind of joke you shouldn't make around Allan."

"You liked it."

"I had a weak moment." She combed her fingers through his hair and his body instantly contracted.

Each time she touched him, his skin grew more sensitive. He took a deep breath, trying to focus on something else.

"What did the rug say to the floor?" he asked.

She sighed as her scissors cut across the first lock of hair. "Please don't. I'm holding something sharp."

"No. That's not it."

"Striker…"

"It said, don't move. I've got you covered."

She groaned.

Striker wanted to groan, too. The stupid jokes weren't distracting him. But her breasts sure were.

They jiggled gently in his peripheral vision. Her knees just barely brushed his rib cage. And her breath whooshed softly against his skin.

His scalp tingled with heat where her fingertips brushed it, systematically lifting sections of his hair. The snip, snip of the scissors echoed in his ear, while her sweet breath tantalized him.

For better or worse, she was turning him on.

Seriously.

He reminded himself that she was more tart than sweet and, if not for this crazy meeting-Allan mission, she was hardly likely to give him the time of day.

But when she leaned over to blow the fine cut hairs from the back of his neck, he felt a shot of raw arousal burn down to his toes.

This was bad.

He shifted.

"Stay still or you'll have a bald spot," she warned.

He stopped moving and gripped the arms of the chair, trying to think about something, anything besides the erotic enigma of Erin.

He fought an urge to reach out and touch her, to draw her into his arms and feel her body mold against his own. He imagined himself whispering something sexy and sweet in her ear. And then he imagined she'd kiss him.

It could work. She was a woman, after all. From L.A. to Singapore, women loved it when a guy got poetic. Maybe she really would kiss him. Couldn't hurt to try.

Striker pulled himself up short. What was he thinking? He was supposed to be a crude, uncouth bohemian. Seductive poetry would hardly be keeping in character.

Erin moved to his front, running her fingertips through his hairline. He closed his eyes again, tightening his grip on the chair, fighting his growing urge to reach for her.

She stepped closer, shifting one leg between his spread knees.

He popped his eyes open.

Was she crazy?

Did she have *no* idea what she was doing to him?

She was a gorgeous woman, touching him intimately, breathing on his skin, her breasts only inches from his face. Unless she was hopelessly naive, she had to know how any man would react. Heck, if he really was the bohemian she thought him, he'd...

Striker paused.

Why not?

It would definitely be keeping in character. And it wasn't like her opinion of him could sink a whole lot lower.

Maybe if he got it over with, he'd stop wondering what her lips tasted like. Then he could focus his mind on other things. Like going back to Seattle tomorrow. And how he was going to deal with his father.

The more he thought about it, the more he realized kissing Erin was an excellent idea.

He'd kiss her, and know for sure what it was like.

She'd probably slap him.

Then he'd swear never to do it again.

End of story.

He squared his shoulders, telling himself to think like an uncouth bohemian.

As soon as she stopped cutting, he reached out and settled his palms on the back of her thighs. No, that was too polite. He slid them firmly up to her rear end, jerking her forward, pulling her down into his lap.

She gasped. "What the—"

"I let you give me the cut," he drawled. "Now it's time to give me a buzz."

ERIN was buzzing.

Seriously, sexually buzzing.

She guessed this must be what happened when you gave in and flirted with a man. Another good reason to nip the flirting habit in the bud.

Running her fingers through Striker's hair had been bad enough. And she'd had a plausible excuse for that. But now his hands were clamped around her hips and his hot, hard thigh was pressing against her rear.

His bare chest was broad, his pecs, biceps and shoulders solid as steel. He'd shaved this morning, giving him an aristocratic look that was definitely at odds with his personality.

His eyes were sky blue and a small white scar slashed through the corner of one dark eyebrow.

Before she could stop herself, she reached out and touched it.

"Bar fight," he said roughly.

She nodded, reminding herself of who he was. But her body didn't seem to care. His husky voice vibrated right through her skin. And the electricity from his heat worked its way along the length of her finger.

He cupped her chin. His touch wasn't particularly gentle. It was confident and purposeful.

She caught her breath, staring into his blue eyes, knowing she should hate this. Knowing she should strenuously object to it. But the turquoise streaks radiating out from the pupils, reflecting the sunlight, hinted at a mystery that fascinated her. And the word *no* got stuck in her throat.

One strong hand slid indolently up the side of her rib cage, thumb barely skimming the edge of her breast as he tipped his head sideways.

Sharp desire pierced her chest. She wished he'd haul her forward and kiss her already. Just get it over with before she came to her senses and told him to back off.

*Kiss me.*

His hand tightened around her rib cage, pulling her toward him. She stopped breathing as inches turned to centimeters, then centimeters turned to millimeters. His lips touched hers and a million fireworks exploded behind her eyes.

A mass of emotion swelled in her chest and she gripped his shoulders, trying to keep the world from tipping on its axis.

His lips hardened. His mouth opened. His arms wrapped fully around her, sliding her body up tight against his bare chest, crushing her breasts, pressing his thigh firmly between her legs.

She opened her mouth, inviting him in, and his tongue tangled with hers. Sensation crested in her body. She wanted nothing more than to get closer and closer.

The amazing kiss went on and on, until he suddenly sucked in a breath and backed off a few millimeters. He reached up and grasped her wrist, gently prying it from his shoulder.

"Ouch," he whispered against her lips.

She opened her eyes.

Her hand still held the small scissors and there was a red gash in Striker's shoulder, blood trickling down his arm.

She sprang back. "Oh, no. Oh, no! I'm *so* sorry!"

He let go of her wrist, flexing his shoulder. "Not a problem."

She scooted to the counter and grabbed a box of tissue. "I *stabbed* you."

"I know. I ignored it for as long as I could."

She blinked as she handed him the tissues.

He'd *ignored it*? He'd had a pair of scissors sticking into his shoulder, but he'd kept on kissing her?

He plucked a couple of tissues from the box and held them against the wound.

Erin shook herself out of her amazement. She gestured to his shoulder. "We need to get you something for that."

"It'll be fine."

"You're bleeding."

"Good thing I took my sweater off."

She frowned. Did he really think she only cared about the sweater? Had she seemed that single-minded?

He shook his head and gave her a small grin. "Erin. That was a joke."

"You need stitches?"

"Hardly. The bleeding'll stop in a minute. How does my hair look?"

Erin felt terrible. "Want me to go get you a mirror?"

"I can walk."

"I'm really sorry."

He stood up. "Don't worry about it. It's just a little cut."

"But—"

Striker cupped her cheek with his palm and gazed deeply into her eyes. "It's barely more than a scratch. And, trust me, it was worth it."

Erin felt her knees go weak.

That was probably the sexiest thing anyone had ever said to her. And it was *Striker* who'd said it.

The front door slammed.

Striker's hand fell away.

Julie breezed into the kitchen wearing a white beach cover-up, her hair in a small, wispy ponytail on the top of her head. Her tan was already starting to darken.

"Not that I'd mind spending the rest of my life here," she said, swinging open the refrigerator door and grabbing a bottle of water. "But have you guys called Allan Baldwin yet?"

She stopped, mid-drink, and stared at Striker. "Nice hair. What's she going to do to you next?"

Striker sputtered out a short laugh. "Quite frankly, I can't wait to find out."

Feeling completely self-conscious, Erin quickly crossed the room and focused on the phone book. "Calling Allan is a good idea."

She'd been distracted there for a minute. But there was no point in putting off the call. If Charles was on the prowl for Allan's contract, they didn't have any time to waste.

Striker sauntered over to the counter, stopping next to Erin, an enigmatic grin on his face. "Whatever you say, boss."

Her embarrassment diminished and annoyance took its place. He must be so proud of himself.

He'd acted like a caveman and she'd responded with enthusiasm. There'd be no living with his ego now.

She took a surreptitious step away from him as she read out the phone number.

Striker dialed.

"Allan Baldwin, please," he said into the receiver.

Erin backed into the counter on the other side of the room, gripping the cool Arborite lip. She was nervous about Allan's reaction, she told herself. The coiled tension in the pit of her stomach had nothing to do with Striker's kiss.

Hoo, boy. She'd kissed Striker.

"Striker Reeves calling," he said.

While he spoke, she focused on his lips, swallowing against a dry throat as her memory kicked in. Okay, chill, it was nothing to get excited about. It hadn't been a long kiss or anything.

Or had it? Truth was, she couldn't quite remember.

"Hey, Allan. How's it going?"

But it was a powerful kiss. There was no denying it was a rock-you-to-your-toes kiss.

And, if she'd sensed that, Striker must have sensed it, too.

She nearly groaned out loud.

"You're right," said Striker. "It has."

She hoped he didn't get any crazy ideas. Like thinking she might want to do it again.

She didn't.

"I'm here on Blue Earth Island."

He was hardly her type.

"With a couple of friends." He smiled at Erin, and her heart rate tripled.

She assured herself it meant nothing.

"We were thinking about stopping by later tonight. If you're going to be around."

Erin stilled.

"Yeah? That'd be great."

She held her breath.

"Seven sounds good. See you then." Striker hung up the phone.

"He said *yes?*" asked Julie.

"He invited us for dinner," said Striker.

Erin felt a stone drop into the middle of her stomach. Forget Striker kissing. Striker with a seafood fork and the wrong wineglass? Maybe tucking his napkin into his collar and taking toothpicks out of his breast pocket?

"You sure you know how to do that?" she asked.

Striker rolled his eyes. "No problem. I've been chowing down my entire life."

*Chowing down?*

Erin straightened away from the counter, no time to dwell on her silly physical response. "I think it's time for drastic action."

# 5

By drastic action, Striker had discovered that Erin meant more etiquette lessons. She'd spent the afternoon introducing him to every utensil known to mankind, and some he was pretty sure she'd made up. *He'd* spent the afternoon pretending to pay attention.

The reality was, all he'd been able to think about was the kiss. Their kiss.

Now, dressed in his new suit, and feeling pretty darned self-satisfied, he smiled to himself as he watched her walk with Julie down the pot-lit pathway toward Allan's front door.

He'd kissed her. And she'd kissed him back.

She hadn't slapped him down. Not by a long shot.

He knew he should feel guilty for misleading her about his identity, but he was too busy savoring the fact that she'd *kissed him back*. Even though she didn't know he was rich, even though she'd never seen his jet, even though she acted like she didn't really like him all that much.

For a sharp-tongued, sassy, confrontational woman, she sure was fun when she let her hair down.

And she was incredible to look at.

Especially from this angle.

Julie had dressed in basic black again. But Erin wore a dusty-rose silk dress with a low, scooped neckline and a matching scarf draped loosely around her neck. The fabric rippled sensuously against her body. Her bare shoulders were smooth as silk, her graceful arms sleek and sexy, and her glossy, wind-blown hair caressed the exposed skin on her back.

Striker could see a thousand places he'd like to kiss her.

He flexed his shoulder. Well, once he disarmed her. He wondered if she'd let him anywhere near her in the foreseeable future.

They climbed the stairs of the huge West Coast–style house and pressed the bell. He half expected a butler to open the door, but it was Allan who greeted them.

Allan immediately grinned and reached out his hand. "Hey, Striker. I can't believe you're on the island. Great to see you again."

Striker shook Allan's hand. "Guy's gotta take a vacation sometime."

"Wouldn't you rather do it in London?"

"I heard Blue Earth Island was the greatest place on earth."

Allan glanced at Julie and his gaze rested there. "You heard right."

"This is Julie Green and Erin O'Connell," said Striker. "They're both friends of mine."

"Great to meet you." Allan took Julie's hand and then Erin's. Then he stepped back into the flagstone foyer, gesturing them inside.

The foyer opened into a cathedral ceilinged living room. Although Striker had visited beautiful homes all his life, he was impressed with this one.

It was open and spacious, with two story glass walls overlooking rocky cliffs that dropped down to a windswept, dusk-darkened coast. Built on a spit of land on the windward point of the island, it was private, ruggedly gorgeous and invitingly comfortable, dotted with West Coast carvings and lit candles.

Allan addressed Julie and Erin as he led them towards two blue-plaid overstuffed couches in a sunken conversation nook where a small fire burned in a stone fireplace. "Are you both from the Seattle area?"

"From New York," said Erin as she sat down.

"Oh." Allan's eyebrows arched. He gestured to Julie to take one end of a couch. "Striker flew you in?"

Erin nodded.

Allan's smile turned contemplative.

Striker paused.

Uh-oh. This was an unexpected curveball.

"Yes, he did," said Erin, not realizing what her answer would mean to Allan.

"Really…" Judging by the slightly amazed edge to Allan's tone, he assumed Erin and Julie were pickups from some New York party—the kind of women Striker usually dated.

Not that Erin and Julie were the kind of women Striker usually dated. In fact, Allan must be pretty impressed with Striker's pickup ability. Good for Striker's reputation, but he somehow doubted Erin would be thrilled.

Allan sat down on the same couch as Julie, a gleam of anticipation in his eyes.

Striker took the seat next to Erin. He couldn't really blame Allan for the assumption. After all, he was well aware of how Striker got his nickname—Striker never struck out.

Too bad he had to set the record straight this time.

"They're both just my *friends*," he told Allan, shooting him a meaningful stare.

Erin gave Striker a puzzled look.

"*Of course*," said Allan, in a tone that told Striker he'd be happy to go along.

Striker didn't know whether to swear or laugh.

"Can I get anybody a drink?" asked Allan, rising. He looked down at Julie first, obviously assuming she was his date. "A cocktail? Some wine?"

"Wine sounds great," she said.

"Red or white?"

"Whatever you have."

He gestured towards a hallway. "Come and take a look in the wine cellar." Then he shifted his attention to Erin and Striker. "Anybody else want a tour?"

Erin moved to get up, but Striker put a hand on her arm.

"You two go ahead and pick something out," he said.

Erin shot him a glare. She hissed under her breath, "What are you—"

"Stay," he warned in an undertone.

She hesitated, obviously wanting to get to know Allan better.

Striker increased the pressure on her arm.

Finally, she spoke out loud, her tone pleasant despite the fact that she had to be annoyed. "You know what I like, right Julie?"

"You bet," said Julie.

Allan smiled and offered Julie his arm.

Striker could only hope he didn't make a pass at her in the wine cellar.

As soon as they were out of sight, Erin rounded on Striker. Her brown eyes flashed, dark and angry. "*What* are you doing?"

"We have to talk," he said.

"About what?"

Striker shifted sheepishly. "We need to come up with a cover story."

"We already *have* a story."

Striker shook his head. "It's not good enough."

"*Now* you tell me this?"

"I didn't realize…"

"Didn't realize *what*?"

He ran his hand through his newly cut hair, shifting his gaze from her face to the fire crackling in the cavernous stone, feeling unaccountably embarrassed about having to explain. "We have to pretend I've known you for a while."

"Why?"

"I, uh, kind of have this reputation…"

A small crease appeared in her forehead. "So?"

He'd never tried to put this delicately before, never felt the need to put it delicately before. "In high school," he began. "I picked up a lot of girls."

She stared at him blankly for a moment. "…and this somehow means I can't go see Allan's wine cellar?"

He cleared his throat. "In high school, I picked up a lot of girls in my Mustang… You know… Then, when I got older, and I got a plane…"

"And…"

"I picked up women."

"You're telling me you're a hound dog?"

Striker shifted, wanting to phrase it differently. But…

Well.

Yeah.

Okay.

Actually, he was.

She glanced at the doorway Julie and Allan had left through. "Do we have to talk about this *now?*"

"Thing is, when you told Allan you flew in with me, he assumed…"

Her eyes went wide in the candlelight. "That we're a couple of your pickups?"

"Yeah. Striker never strikes out."

Erin dropped her forehead into her hands. "Oh, perfect. Just…perfect."

"I think we can fix it," he said.

She shook her head. "*How?* Good grief, I get you to help me so that Allan *won't* think we're coming on to him, and now *this.*"

"We tell him we've known each other for a few months. Convince him we're friends—"

"Instead of temporary lovers?" Her laughter rang hollow.

"Yeah. Basically."

"You think he's going to believe that?" she asked.

"It's not like we are…" Striker remembered the kiss again. His voice dropped. "Lovers, I mean."

She looked up, and the atmosphere shifted, until the kiss hung in the air between them. He swore he could still feel the sweet sensation of her body, and it drowned out everything else.

He wanted to kiss her again. Desperately. And he knew the hunger must be shining in his eyes. If he didn't cut this out, Allan was going to be convinced there was something going on between them.

"The only problem is…" he said.

She shook her head, sighing in disbelief. "The *only* problem?"

"You're beautiful," he whispered.

"You're trouble," she replied.

"Definitely."

"What am I going to do with you?" she asked.

"For starters, don't give me openings like that."

"Striker..."

"Erin..."

"This morning..."

"Happened," he said. "And there's no point in pretending it didn't."

"It was just a kiss, you know. It didn't mean anything."

Striker paused, gazing at her creamy soft skin in the flickering firelight. "If it didn't mean anything," he said. "I wouldn't be trouble."

She didn't deny it. Just stared at him long enough to jump-start his libido. And he was seriously thinking about kissing her again here and now.

She blinked and straightened. "Okay, where did we meet?"

"Huh?"

"Our cover story. Where are we going to tell Allan we met?"

Striker batted down his desire. "New York," he answered. "Keep it simple."

"Have you been there?"

"Yes. I have."

"Where in New York?"

"The River Café."

"You've been *there?*"

Striker hesitated. "I've seen it on TV."

Erin nodded.

Julie's laughter sounded from the hallway.

"We picked a merlot and a Beaujolais," said Allan, holding up two bottles as they entered the living room. "The cook's barbecuing filet mignon."

STRIKER WAS a hound dog. Why did that not surprise Erin?

It fit with everything else she knew about him. And it proved the only reason his kiss felt special was that he'd practiced it on dozens, maybe hundreds of women. No wonder his lips had just the right pressure, not too dry, not too moist, warm, tingly, minty fresh.

Well, now that she'd learned his little secret, it was definitely going to be a whole lot easier to ignore him. Take now, he was sitting right beside her at a small, round table in the apex of Allan's two glass walls, and she barely even knew he was there.

The steaks were perfect, the wine superb, and the view of the lit yard was magnificent. And she was taking full advantage of her big opportunity with Allan because she was no longer worried about Striker getting under her skin. He was just a man, a convenience to her current purpose. Nothing more.

"…that's when I met Erin in New York," he said to Allan.

Erin mentally braced herself, keeping her features even, trying to keep her expression from giving away their lies.

Allan frowned and turned to look at Julie. "I thought you said you met him on Monday?"

"She did," Striker put in smoothly. "It was Erin that I met in New York."

Julie shot Erin an incredulous look.

Striker turned to Erin, tapping his index finger against his wineglass. "Where was it? That little restaurant just over the Brooklyn Bridge..."

Erin took her cue. "The River Café."

Julie's eyes widened.

Striker snapped his fingers. "That was it. You had the duck, but I couldn't convince you to go for the crème brûlée." He returned his attention to Allan. "Derek introduced us."

Julie continued to stare at Erin, biting down on her bottom lip in an obvious attempt to mask a smile. Oh, sure, she'd love this. Despite Erin's determination to guard her ethics, she was stuck playing along with the lies that rolled off Striker's tongue.

Thank goodness Julie didn't know he'd kissed her.

Allan refilled the wineglasses. "How are your brothers doing?" he asked Striker.

"Tyler just got married," said Striker.

"Really?"

Striker nodded. "In July."

"What about Derek?"

"Derek? Not married." Striker shook his head and both men chuckled. "I doubt there's a woman alive who'd take him on."

"I'm surprised he hasn't—"

"What about you?" asked Striker. "Tell me about your diamonds."

Erin quickly kicked him under the table. She couldn't believe he'd blurted that out.

She'd planned to fake an epiphany moment later on. She could see it all now: "Oh, you're *that* Allan Baldwin. What an unexpected surprise. Julie and I are in the gem business…"

But how was she going to fake surprise if Striker started talking about diamonds right off the bat?

Striker didn't flinch from her kick. He didn't even look her way.

Allan cupped his wineglass and swirled the merlot, gazing into the candle flame for a moment. "It's not the diamonds we're excited about this week." He leaned forward, voice dropping conspiratorially. "In fact, I just heard from the assayer on the Green Ice property."

"Make sure you don't give us any state secrets," said Striker, a warning edge to his tone.

Erin kicked him again. Quite frankly, she was curious as all get out about the state secrets of Allan's new emerald mine.

"Portal number forty-four is showing some serious gem-quality stones," said Allan. "They've come up with a few flawless and a Trapiche."

Julie jerked straight up. "You mined a Trapiche outside of Colombia?"

Allan nodded.

"How is that possible?" she asked.

Striker leaned over to whisper in Erin's ear. "Kick me one more time and I'll make you kiss it better."

The image gave Erin a little shiver. She tamped it down.

"Carbon," said Allan.

"But..." ventured Julie.

"You know your emeralds," he said.

Julie obviously regrouped. Taking a sip of her wine, she blinked guilelessly. "I really like jewelry."

"It's rough. But do you want to see it?"

Julie coughed, then sputtered. So much for regrouping. "It's *here?*"

"In my safe."

"Will you marry me?"

Allan grinned and gently tapped the bottom of her chin with his index finger as he stood up, dropping his napkin onto the tablecloth. "Now there's an offer I don't get everyday. Be right back."

As soon as he was gone, Erin turned on Striker. "What do you think you're doing?"

"Me doing? You're the one beating the crap out of my shins."

"You asked him about his diamonds." She couldn't believe it.

"So?"

"So, now I either have to cough up who we are right away or get even more tangled up in lies I won't know how to get out of."

"So, cough."

"I can't."

"Why not?"

"That's not part of the plan. We've barely met him. And now there's the emeralds. I don't even know what terms I can offer him for the emeralds. I have to talk to my boss. I have to—"

"Uh, guys?" Julie interrupted, quickly glancing at the door Allan had left through. "Not that this isn't the single greatest moment of my life, seeing his Trapiche and all—"

Striker clamped his hand around Erin's wrist and included Julie in his hard stare. "You two can *not* use anything you learn from Allan under these circumstances. About a Trapiche or anything else."

Erin was insulted. "What? You think I'm going to rush out and indulge in a little insider trading?"

Julie cleared her throat. "Before Allan gets back, I think you two better tell me why you lied about meeting in New York."

"I need your word," Striker growled. There was an underlying hardness in his expression, an astuteness she never would have imagined. "Both of you. You can't use anything you learn before he knows who you are."

"New York?" Julie prompted.

"Your word," said Striker.

"Fine. Yes. Of course you have our word. I'm a buyer not an investor."

He let go of Erin's wrist and she turned to Julie.

"We lied because Allan thought we were Striker's pickups. Turns out Striker had quite a reputation in high school."

Julie quirked one eyebrow. "Oh. I guess that explains the wine cellar."

Erin sat back. "What happened in the wine cellar?"

Before Julie could do more than smile secretively, Allan came back into the room.

He opened a blue velvet case and held it in front of Julie. "You are the first people outside the company to see this. They also sent down a couple of the bigger flawless."

"My kingdom for a loupe," breathed Julie, reaching out to reverently touch the stones, obviously dying to examine them more closely.

"You should seriously consider a rich husband," said Allan.

Julie looked up at him, eyes sparking with mischief beneath her thick lashes. "I am."

Allan smiled back at her, chuckling low as he handed the velvet box to Erin and Striker.

Erin wasn't as much of an expert as Julie, but she'd been around enough stones in her life to know greatness when she saw it. Allan's diamonds were acknowledged as spectacular. His emeralds were going to set the world on its ear.

She knew she should tell him they were from Elle. But she needed some time to think strategically. She absolutely could *not* blow this opportunity. If she didn't get in on the ground floor of North America's first major emerald find, Patrick would have her shot at sunrise.

"Coffee on the patio?" asked Allan.

Striker handed him back the gems. "Sounds good to me."

Allan pulled out Julie's chair. He put his hand on the small of her back as they strolled toward the glass doors, heads bent together, talking.

Striker pulled out Erin's chair. "I think you'd better tell him," he singsonged in her ear.

She shook her head. "Not yet."

"You're going to get yourself in trouble."

She stood. "I have to talk to Patrick first. My boss."

"I'm no expert—"

"An important point."

"But it seems to me that, in order for this to work, Allan has to trust you."

"He will."

Striker settled his hand in the small of her back. "You're not making it easy for him."

She tried to ignore the hand. He was just copying Allan, trying to play the classy gentleman.

"Nothing in life is easy," she said. "It's a balancing act. Total honesty versus strategic interests."

The pressure of his hand increased and his voice suddenly sounded far away. "You sure got that right."

# 6

TOTAL HONESTY versus strategic interest.

Striker mulled those profound words as he watched Erin move around the dim kitchen. They'd walked home from Allan's along the beach, then Julie had decided to take a shower.

Erin had decided to make some coffee.

Striker had decided to watch her.

She'd taken off her silk scarf, and the dress shimmered pearlescent in the moonlight against her pale skin. It hugged every curve and hollow, setting off her dark eyes. Her bare feet were soundless as she padded from the cupboard to the counter and back again.

"You want to hear something totally honest?" he asked.

She turned to look at where he was leaned against the doorjamb, arms folded across his chest.

"Sure."

"You're gorgeous in the moonlight."

A half smile played at her lips. "That sounded more like a strategic interest than total honesty."

He straightened and took a couple of steps toward her. "You think?"

"I think."

"Okay, I'll play along. Tell me what my strategic interests are."

She set the glass pot down in the coffeemaker and leaned back against the counter, bracing her hands on either side, bringing the dress up tight across her breasts. "That's easy. What you're always after. You forget, your reputation precedes you."

Striker chuckled, drawing closer. "Good point. Did I mention that I never strike out?"

"So I hear."

"There's a reason for that, you know."

"Do tell."

Striker paused. So much for total honesty. Truth was, he had a really great jet, a Mustang convertible and several million dollars in his bank account. He'd never tried to pick up a woman without them.

"I'm a good-lookin', smooth-talkin' love machine," he drawled, moving closer, trying to sound crude and classless.

"Please tell me that line doesn't work on real women."

"I don't know. I've never tried it before."

"Give me one of your real lines."

*Want to take a ride in my jet?* Good lord, had he really used that so shamelessly?

After a moment, she tipped her head to one side. "Go on. Give me your best shot."

Striker tried, but for the life of him, he couldn't think of a pickup line that didn't involve material goods. Out of desperation, he settled on the truth.

"You're the most beautiful woman I've ever met."

"Not very original."

He paused right in front of her, letting his fingertips brush lightly against hers. "But it's a classic if you say it with total honesty."

"Problem is, I've seen how well you lie."

"Another good point." He leaned in, gazing deep into her eyes. "But you truly are the most beautiful woman I've ever met."

"It won't work, Striker."

"It won't?"

"I'm onto you. So, unless you want to give up your nickname in abject defeat, you'd better not even try me."

Striker backed off a few inches and folded his arms over his chest. He knew he should leave her alone, but her confidence challenged him on a visceral level. "*Abject defeat?*"

"You bet." She turned slightly to open a foil bag of coffee, her elbow coming into contact with his chest.

He knew he was probably crowding her, but he liked being up close. "You sound pretty sure of yourself."

"Totally."

Striker shrugged. "Okay then. You win."

She turned to look at him. "Just like that?"

"Disappointed?"

"Surprised."

He lifted the coffee scoop out of her hand and chucked her gently under the chin. "Why don't you sit down? You look tired. I can make this."

"Really?"

"Sure."

"Thanks."

Erin padded across the kitchen and sat down on one of the chairs.

Striker started scooping the coffee grounds into the machine, trying not to smile smugly.

Give up on Erin that easily? He didn't think so. One, he was dying to share another dynamite kiss with her. Two, they didn't call him Striker for nothing. And, three, he refused to believe it was all about material goods.

At least not every time.

And here was his big chance to prove that.

First secret of all fail-safe seductions was to throw a woman off guard, make sure she wasn't expecting it.

He finished scooping the coffee grounds and folded the top of the foil pouch. Then he closed the basket and flipped the switch. "What's a tree's favorite drink?"

Julie walked through the doorway wearing a white fluffy robe, her hair wrapped up in a towel. "What?" she asked.

"Don't encourage him," said Erin.

"*Root beer,*" said Striker.

Julie giggled as she sat down.

Erin groaned.

Leaving the coffee to brew, Striker pulled up a third chair. "So, you two happy with the way tonight went?"

"Allan said *yes* to dinner tomorrow," said Erin.

"And you agreed to stay an extra day," Julie said to Striker, eyes twinkling. "Reminds me of double dating in high school."

"It's not a date," said Erin primly. "It's a business dinner."

"You going to tell Allan that?" asked Striker.

"I'll tell him as soon as the opportunity presents itself," she said.

"Don't wait too long."

Instead of responding, Erin turned to Julie. "I need to call Patrick tomorrow morning and tell him about the emeralds. You should give him the technical details."

"I believe the technical term is *holy crap!*"

Erin smiled. "I'll try to remember that." She pushed her hair behind her shoulders. The motion dislodged one of the straps on her dress. It slipped down to loop along her arm.

Striker's throat suddenly went dry and he jumped up from his chair. "Either of you want coffee?"

If he was going to take this seduction slow and subtle, he needed to keep his hands busy.

"Sounds great," said Julie.

"Yes, please," said Erin.

He forced himself to walk away from the table, focusing determinedly on the coffeemaker. He wanted to taste that shoulder—desperately wanted to taste that shoulder. But he couldn't push it. He had to take his time, get it right, make sure she thought it was all her idea.

"Sugar and cream?" he asked as he located some stoneware mugs in a cupboard.

Both the women took it black, so he filled the mugs and carried them over to the table.

"Mmm," Julie sighed. "I'm starting to feel more civilized again. Remind me *never* to hike down a beach in high heels."

"Why didn't you say something?" asked Striker. "I would have called a taxi."

"And miss the extra time with Allan?" asked Erin. "Do you think we're wimps?"

Julie reached down to rub her bare calf. "I am officially a wimp."

"Sore feet?" asked Striker, willing her to say yes.

"I don't know which was worse, walking in my heels or taking them off and exfoliating my feet to within an inch of their life."

Striker held out his hand. "Here. Give me a foot."

"You want my foot?"

"Yeah. I took a reflexology course. I'll make a new woman of you."

Julie brightened. "Really?"

Striker nodded.

She lifted a foot into his lap.

He could not have scripted this better. Once Julie had broken the ice, Erin's feet were all but his.

He stroked up the center of her sole with his thumb and Julie moaned.

He silently thanked her for her support. "Relax ma'am, I'm a professional."

He took a surreptitious glance at Erin, hoping to see a covetous look in her eyes.

No such luck.

She was focused on her coffee cup. "What are we going to cook for Allan tomorrow?"

"Can we microwave?" asked Julie.

Erin shook her head. "We want to impress him, remember?"

"What about a restaurant?" asked Striker.

Again, Erin shook her head. "We need privacy."

"Hire a cook?" asked Julie.

"No time," said Erin.

"I make a great salmon in dill sauce," said Striker.

Erin shot him a surprised and impressed look. "You know how to cook?"

Truth was, salmon in dill sauce was the only thing he'd ever bothered to learn. But women liked a man who was handy in the kitchen, so he nodded. "Love to cook."

"I vote for salmon in dill sauce," said Julie on an-

other moan. "By the way, if I hadn't already pro-
posed to Allan tonight, I'd be proposing to you
right now."

Striker switched feet. "What? You have a rule
about two proposals in one night?"

Julie closed her eyes and sighed in bliss. "Tragi-
cally, yes."

Again, Striker glanced at Erin, hoping to see some
small reaction to his flirting with Julie. Maybe jealousy?

Nothing.

Ah, well. Flirting with another woman wasn't a
particularly highly recommended method of seduction anyway. The foot massage, however, had a near
perfect record.

He redoubled his efforts on Julie and was re-
warded with another moan.

Surely that got Erin's attention.

Apparently not. She stood up, glancing around
the kitchen. "If I find some paper for a list, will you
tell me the salmon ingredients?"

Hmm. He'd never had a seduction victim make a
grocery list before. Though there was that one
woman who dashed out to buy whipped cream.

"Sure," he answered, moving the massage up to
Julie's calves. He figured that way it wouldn't look
so suspicious when he went for Erin's calves.

Erin headed for the living room.

"If I didn't know better," said Julie, from beneath
her lashes, "I'd think you were trying to seduce me."

Striker gave her a lazy smile. "What makes you think I'm not?"

"You don't strike me as the ménage à trois type."

"*Excuse* me?"

"You practically vibrate when Erin's in the room."

And here he thought he was being so subtle. "Don't be ridiculous."

"Hey, it's okay by me. Personally, I think Erin could use a walk on the wild side."

Striker quirked his eyebrows. He'd never been anyone's wild side before.

"She's way too focused on work," said Julie.

"She is?"

"I'm here for the fun. She wouldn't even be here if it weren't for the promotion opportunity."

"Corporate climber?"

"It's the respect she craves. Erin's all about respect."

Striker nodded. "What about you? You get a promotion out of this?"

"Mine's a technical job. I'm not in the line of succession."

"But Erin is?"

"You bet." Julie wiggled her toes. "What about you?"

He glanced up.

Her smiled turned secretive. "What is it you really do?"

Striker's hands slowed. "What do you mean?"

She nodded toward his necktie. "That's a hell of a

sharp Windsor knot. You knew a good year for Beaujolais. And you didn't screw up the silverware once."

"Erin's a good teacher," he said.

"And the tie?"

Striker glanced down. "Debate club."

"*Right,*" she drawled.

Erin breezed back into the room. "Found some paper. I saw a nice fish market down by the coffee shop." She dropped into the chair and started scribbling.

Striker glanced worriedly at Julie.

She smiled and made a zipping motion across her lips.

"OKAY." ERIN looked up from the list to see Striker still working on Julie's feet. She absently rubbed one sole against the inside of her calf. "Salad from the market. We can pick up some French bread and a cake from the bakery. Now, what's in the salmon sauce?"

Julie slipped her foot from Striker's lap. "I'm beat," she said. "You two mind finishing?"

"No problem," said Striker.

"Of course not," said Erin.

He turned to look at her. "Your turn."

"My turn for what?"

"Give me your foot."

Her stomach contracted with a combination of apprehension and anticipation.

Julie stood up. "Go for it. He will make a new woman out of you."

Striker's mouth quirked for a split second.

Erin wanted to. She really did.

Striker reached forward and cupped his palm behind one of her knees. "Give me your foot or I won't tell you the ingredients."

"Why is everything an ultimatum with you?" But she didn't fight him as he levered her bare foot into his lap.

"It's because you're so damn stubborn."

Julie waggled her fingers in a little wave as she headed for the door. "Night kids."

Striker started the massage with a firm stroke of his thumb up the center of Erin's sole. The sensation was so exquisite, she had to bite back a moan.

He stroked again, and she quietly gasped. "First ingredient?"

"Butter," he said mildly.

"Right." She jotted it down.

"Cream," he said, changing the motion of his thumb to draw small circles on the balls of her feet. She could feel the satisfying muscular throb pulsate all the way up her leg.

"Got it," she muttered, her eyelids beginning to grow heavy.

"Dill weed."

Her handwriting was getting shaky and she didn't

quite trust her voice. She nodded and scratched something down on the paper.

"White wine."

She let her eyes flutter closed. "Hmm."

He moved to her heel and did double strokes with both thumbs.

Erin felt herself slide down in her chair. "You ever do this professionally?"

"Nope."

"You'd make a fortune."

He hit a point just below her big toe and she twitched.

"Feel that?" he asked.

"Mmm, hmm."

"You've got a headache, don't you?"

How had he known that? "It's just stress."

He rubbed the same spot again, more gently this time.

Erin felt a warm tingle at the back of her neck.

"You'd be amazed at what reflexology can do. Do you mind if I move you?" His hands stilled.

Erin popped one eye open. She almost begged him to keep rubbing. "What do you mean?"

He set her foot down on the floor and stood up. "Come on." He scooped one arm beneath her knees and wrapped the other around her back.

"Wha…" She clutched his neck as he started to lift her.

He straightened to full height. "This is going to

work way better on the couch. You need a pillow under your neck so you can relax it."

"Oh. Okay." If it meant he was going to keep up the foot massage, she was game.

He crossed the living room and laid her down on a couch in front of the picture window.

"Can you see the stars?" he asked as he settled a pillow behind her head.

"Yes."

"Good." He dimmed the lights, then he lit a couple of candles. "You want music or quiet?"

"Quiet," she said.

He moved to the other end of the couch, sat down and lifted her feet into his lap, gently picking up the massage where he left off. "It's very important that you keep your neck relaxed, or this isn't going to work."

"Okay." She wasn't about to argue with Striker and his magic fingers.

As he worked the tension out of her muscles, Erin let her whole body relax into his touch. Her eyes lost focus until the stars above were blurry points of light in a purple haze.

Striker tirelessly massaged her feet, covering all points from her knees to her baby toes, but always coming back to the headache spot. Gradually, it subsided to a dull throb. She'd known it would go away eventually, they always did. But it was still a huge relief.

"Is it gone?" he whispered.

"Almost."

He slipped out from under her feet, crouching down near her head. "Turn over."

She opened her eyes and gazed into his face, only inches away in the flickering candlelight. He was an incredibly handsome man.

Of course, her opinion could be slightly skewed at the moment, since right now he was her favorite person on the planet. She could definitely understand why Julie had talked about proposing.

"What for?" she asked.

"I know a neck massage that will make you one hundred percent pain free."

That sounded glorious to Erin. "Why are you doing this?"

He made a rolling motion with his index finger. "Turn over. Doing what?"

She struggled for the right words as she moved onto her stomach on the soft couch cushions. "You know… Taking care of me."

He chuckled. "Why wouldn't I?"

Her voice was muffled against the cushion. "I haven't been the easiest person to get along with."

"You're under stress. Besides, I'm hoping you'll be nicer once your headache's gone."

She couldn't help but chuckle. "I wouldn't count on that. I've only had the headache for a couple of hours."

"I'm an optimist." He pressed his fingertips into the corded muscles at the base of her skull.

"Ouch."

"Relax."

"I'm trying."

"Your muscles have tightened up around your nerves and blood vessels. If we can get them to relax, the pain will go away."

"Are you a doctor as well as a pilot?"

"Definitely not. But I've played doctor once or twice."

"Once or twice? You're far too modest."

His low laugh vibrated right through her. "Busted," he whispered. "Enough about me. Tell me how you ended up in diamonds."

"I majored in economics, minored in geology."

"Was it your plan to get into the jewelry business?"

Erin shook her head.

"Stay relaxed," he admonished, moving his thumbs down her neck, working his way out toward her shoulders, drawing ever-widening circles over her tight muscles.

"There was a job ad in the classifieds, and I applied."

"Simple as that?"

She started to nod, then stopped herself. "Simple as that. Who knew I'd love it so much?"

"What appeals to you about it?" he asked.

"What doesn't? I get to travel, meet exciting people, make deals that help our designers create masterpieces. I help people celebrate the greatest joys of their lives."

"Sounds like you picked the right profession."

"Definitely."

He stretched the thumb circles down between her shoulder blades, hitting on a particularly sore muscle.

She moaned.

"Hurt?"

"It tightens up whenever I spend too much time on the computer."

He made his way around the edges of the knot, gradually working out the tension until she felt as though she might melt into a pool of jelly and ooze onto the floor.

"Erin?" he whispered close to her ear.

His breath was hot against her skin and she could imagine his lips brushing against her, kissing her ever so gently.

She subconsciously stretched toward him. "Yes?"

"You be okay if I go a little lower?" He tugged at the straps of her dress.

"Sure." *Yes. Anything. Just don't stop.*

He pushed the straps down her arms and eased her dress down a few inches. "Stay on your stomach."

She nodded.

He inched it a little further. The neckline rasped its way over her nipples and she sucked in a breath.

"Okay?" he asked.

"Fine," she all but squeaked.

Her skin had turned supersensitive and she had a crystal-clear vision of his rough hands on her breasts.

He went back to the sore spot between her shoulder blades, then gradually worked his way down her spine. His fingertips were strong and sure. Her muscles couldn't decide whether to relax in ecstasy or tighten with arousal.

She filled her lungs, suddenly attuned to his scent. The candles flickered warmly off the wood walls, bathing the room in a golden glow. His fingertips moved lower, firmer, deeper.

Erin didn't know what heaven felt like, but she was pretty sure it had to be close to this. Her body began to tingle and her thighs began to twitch.

His warm breath caressed her skin.

His lips would be next.

She was sure his lips would be next.

She couldn't be the only one feeling the heady press of the passion rising between them. He couldn't be doing all this to her and not know it.

His touch skimmed the top of her buttocks, and his breathing grew deeper and faster.

Was that a sign?

Was he feeling something, too?

He had to be.

*Kiss me. Kiss me. Kiss me.*

She waited, barely breathing. But he just kept massaging.

She turned her head and whispered his name into the sultry darkness.

"Hmm?"

Her gaze sought and caught his.

His hands stilled. His eyes were burning with passion, midnight-blue, dark with need.

Without giving herself a chance for second thoughts, she flipped onto her back.

Striker stared at her for the space of a single heartbeat, eyes darting to her breasts and then back to her lips. Then he swooped down and his hot lips settled on hers.

The kiss was everything she remembered, everything she'd imagined, everything she'd ever wanted.

She wrapped her arms around his neck and arched up to complete it.

He slipped his strong forearms around the small of her back and pulled her against him. He angled into the kiss, opening wide, thrusting his tongue into her mouth as if he couldn't get close enough.

Fine with her. She wanted him against her, around her, inside her. An avalanche of desire was thundering through her body, demanding satisfaction.

His kisses grew hotter, molten, consuming. He kissed her lips, her neck, her cheeks, her eyes, laving her skin with his tongue then caressing it with his soft lips.

He nibbled his way along one ear and she gasped his name out loud.

"You're delicious," he rumbled.

He slid one hand between their bodies, cupping

her breast with the searing heat of his palm. He tested her nipple between his thumb and forefinger.

Blasts of desire spiraled into her system.

She needed to get closer, needed to feel his skin against hers. She reached for the knot in his tie, fumbling.

"Striker?" she begged for help.

# 7

STRIKER REACHED FOR his tie and yanked it loose, pulling it off over his head and dropping it. It slithered down to pile between Erin's creamy, soft breasts. The sight nearly undid him.

He ripped at the buttons of his shirt, quickly shrugging his way out of it so he could feel her breasts against his bare skin. She was soft and warm, and silky smooth.

He pulled her up tight, nearly crushing the breath out of her, kissing the gasp of surprise from her mouth. Even as he curled his tongue around hers, he tried to tell himself to slow down, back off a little and quit acting like a teenager. But it was no good.

He hoped her gasps meant she was keeping pace.

He kissed her long and hot and hard because he couldn't get enough of her lips. They were tender, delicious, sexy as hell. His hand cupped her breast, and he wanted to pull back and stare, take in all of her beauty.

But pulling back meant breaking the kiss, and his lips wouldn't let him do that just yet. Maybe they never would.

She arched her back and he couldn't resist tasting more of her body.

He worked his way down her neck, peppering wet kisses over the mound of her breast, making his way to her hardened nipples. He covered one with his mouth, his heat against the cool of her delicate skin. He swirled his tongue around her and she moaned his name, fingers tunneling into his hair.

He felt an immense jolt of satisfaction crest within him. She wanted him.

For the first time in his life, a woman wanted him and him alone. Erin didn't know about his wealth, his family, his possessions.

He wanted to shout from a rooftop.

He moved to her other breast, while his hands slid down her arched back, kneading their way over her buttocks.

"Striker," she gasped.

"Erin," he answered.

"I want you."

"Me, too."

"Now," she said.

"Oh, yeah."

He clasped her skimpy panties and yanked them down her legs. "Erin," he breathed again, looking his fill, unable to believe she was lying with him, beautiful, sexy, amazing.

He slid one hand up her smooth legs, along her calf, past the tender skin behind her knee, absorbing her satin feel as he gazed deeply into her bottomless eyes.

When he reached her searing heat, her eyes fluttered closed and her lips softened on an expressed sigh.

"Yes," she whispered, flexing her hips, giving herself thoroughly and totally to him.

A wave of tender emotion poured through Striker, unlike anything he'd ever experienced before. Not making love, not flying, not with anyone, ever.

She was like no other woman he'd ever met.

She was special.

And he'd treat her...

Striker stilled, something cold and heavy settling on his chest.

Treat her like what? The same way he'd treated every other woman in his life? The chill spread out through his body.

What the *hell* did he think he was doing?

"Striker?" Her voice seemed to come from far away.

He wanted to kick himself. He was making love to her under false pretenses. He'd just spent two hours devoted to a callused and calculated seduction.

And, if that wasn't bad enough. He'd lied to her.

She thought he was an ordinary charter pilot. She had no idea that his seduction techniques had been perfected on six continents.

He'd treated sex as a game. Just like he always did. Only this time it was worse. He'd stacked the deck.

He gazed at her with aching regret—her beautiful hair, her creamy smooth skin, her dark, pouty lips.

Though it was the hardest thing he'd ever done, he forced himself to let go. He pulled back, thumping down onto the floor beside the couch, clenching his fists.

"Striker?" Her eyes were full of confusion.

"I'm *so* sorry," he said, looking away, not trusting himself.

"About what?"

"This." He spread his hands wide and squeezed his eyes shut.

She gave a nervous laugh. "I, uh, really don't think *this* was anything to be—"

"You were right about me," he said, forcing himself to look her in the eyes. "More right than you'll ever know."

"I…was?" She inched her dress down her thighs.

He hardened his voice. It was better if she hated him. "I'm pond scum."

Her eyes narrowed. "Don't you think that's a little harsh?"

"I seduced you, Erin."

She adjusted the top of her dress, covering her breasts. Thank goodness for small mercies.

"Well, yes," she said. "But you did have a little help."

"You don't understand." He shook his head and dragged his hand through his hair, pressing his fingertips hard against his scalp. What was the matter with him? Why had he done this to her?

"It didn't just happen," he confessed, refusing to give himself any quarter. "This whole thing was a calculated, deliberate lie."

"What whole thing?" The confusion in her voice was turning to frustration.

Good. He'd much rather have her mad than hurt.

"What are you talking about?" she asked.

"The coffee," he admitted. "Julie's massage. The salmon—"

"You lied about the salmon?"

"What? No."

She sat up, seeming to regroup. "Well, thank goodness for that."

"Erin."

"Striker."

"I'm really—"

She cut him off with the palm of her hand. "Listen. I don't know what happened to change your mind, but—"

"I *didn't* change my mind." He reeled at the very thought. "My God, Erin. Do you think I'm not—"

Her voice went cold. "Hey, I was still kissing, and you were stopping. In my book—"

"I stopped because I don't deserve you. Didn't you listen to what I said? This whole thing was a setup."

"You mean the massage wasn't about curing my headache?"

"Well…" Yeah. Actually, he'd cared very much about curing her headache, and it *certainly* hadn't been dependant upon having sex with her later. Still. His primary motive had been to seduce her.

"I see," she said, and the last speck of warmth went out of her eyes.

He stood up and paced across the room to get rid of his pent up energy. "You know how you think I'm an uncouth lowlife?"

She snapped the straps of her dress back onto her shoulders. "Well, if you're trying to change my mind about that—"

"I'm not." Striker drew in a ragged breath. He suddenly felt as if he were looking at himself through his father's eyes, and he sure didn't like what he saw. "I'm trying to tell you that I'm the very worst kind uncouth lowlife. I'm an uncouth lowlife with charm."

"Oh, this is definitely charming."

"I'm sorry."

"If you weren't interested, why did you bother to seduce me?"

Striker bent and picked up his discarded tie, bunching it into his fist. Why? Because she was gorgeous? Because she was sexy? Because she was a challenge? Because he had no morals?

There were a thousand reasons.

"Because I like you," he said.

"Oh, that makes perfect sense."

He didn't answer.

She took a deep breath. "So, why did you stop?"

"Because I like you more than I thought."

She was silent for a minute, her gaze focused on a point somewhere behind his right ear. "Right."

"Erin, I…"

She lifted her chin. "Forget it. Are you staying for dinner tomorrow or not?"

Striker paused. Okay, change the subject. Shut up already and quit embarrassing her.

"Yes," he answered. Running out on her now would only compound his sins.

ERIN WAITED until Striker's bedroom door clicked shut before she slumped back on the couch, pushing her tangled hair back from her face. This was definitely not one of her ego's finest moments.

Her headache was completely gone, but her body still buzzed with sexual arousal. Striker might have changed his mind, but Erin's hormones were on high alert.

She rose unsteadily to her feet, blowing out the candles as she made her way toward the stairs.

Then, having second thoughts, she detoured through the kitchen and grabbed a bottle of brandy and a glass. Maybe she'd take a long, hot bath and deaden her insecurities with liquor.

It wasn't like she had to get up early. The phone call to Patrick would wait, and they had the whole day to plan dinner for Allan.

Besides, her ego needed some serious attention here. She'd been naked and moaning in Striker's arms, and he'd walked away. Left her high and dry. As if she were of no interest to him whatsoever.

Ouch.

Bottle and glass dangling from her fingers, she headed up the stairs.

As she rounded the corner at the top, Julie's door cracked open. "Erin?"

"Yeah?"

"You alone?"

"Yeah."

Julie opened the door wider. "You heading for his room?"

Erin shook her head, resisting an urge to laugh darkly.

Julie stepped back and motioned Erin into her room. "What happened?" she whispered as she closed the door behind them, glancing at the brandy bottle and the single glass.

"It's a little embarrassing," said Erin.

Julie's expression turned to one of animated interest. "Oh, good." She quickly scooped a water glass from the corner table, settling into one of the big armchairs. "Have a seat, pour me a drink and dish."

With a sigh of resignation, Erin curled up in the other chair and splashed a generous drink into each of their glasses. It was hard to know if the gratification of trashing Striker to Julie would be worth the humiliation of telling the story.

"Give," said Julie.

"You have to promise not to laugh."

"Why would I laugh?"

"And you can't pity me, either."

Julie took a drink. "Oh, this is sounding better and better all the time." She wiggled up to the edge of the seat, leaning toward Erin. "Talk, woman."

Erin reminded herself that there was a ninth floor office with her name on it back in New York. Once this was over, it would all be worth it.

Julie knew most of her deep, dark secrets anyway.

"You remember the foot massage?" she asked.

"Do I ever," said Julie, her smile turning dreamy.

Erin took a bracing sip of the brandy. It burned down her throat in a satisfying way. Striker would be a fuzzy memory in no time.

She set the glass down. "Well, the foot massage turned into a neck massage, which turned into a back massage, which turned into a kiss..." She picked up her glass again and studied the amber liquid.

"Doesn't sound too embarrassing so far," said Julie.

"Then he backed off."

Julie leaned farther forward, peeking around the glass. "What do you mean backed off?"

"*Backed* off."

Julie's eyes narrowed. "Did you say *no*?"

Erin shook her head. As a matter of fact, she'd said *yes* in as many ways as she knew how.

"Are you sure?" asked Julie.

Erin tossed back the rest of her drink, clacked the glass down on the table and looked Julie in the eye. "I believe my exact words were 'Striker. I want you. Now.'"

And she had. She still did. How the hell could he *do* this to her?

Julie polished off the last of her brandy and held out her glass for more. "A little hard to misinterpret that."

Erin topped them both up. "I'm guessing. Yeah."

"I could have sworn he was hot for you."

"Apparently not."

"Did he tell you why? Like, is he a religious fanatic or something?"

"He said he liked me."

Julie nodded. "Ahh." Then she shook her head and giggled into her hand. "That makes no sense at all."

"I have a feeling he meant 'like' as in 'respect.'"

"What? He thinks nice girls don't have sex?"

"That's the only explanation I can come up with. I'm pretty sure he was into it. I mean… Okay, I'll say it. I'm *sure* he was into it." Erin shifted in her chair. "They ought to write a law against turning a woman on and then leaving her flat."

"If you thought he was into it, believe me, he was into it," said Julie. "Maybe he's got a 1950s morality thing going."

"Or maybe I don't turn him on all that much," said Erin, experiencing an uncomfortable moment of doubt. Could she have imagined his interest? She had sort of made the first move. What if he was just being polite?

"Oh yeah, that's likely." Julie lifted her index finger from the glass and pointed at Erin. "Trust me, when he was massaging me, he was warming up for you."

Julie's words and the brandy combined to make Erin feel better. She allowed herself a small smile. "You think?"

"I *know.* Whatever's bothering him, it's not that you don't turn him on."

Julie was such a good friend.

It made Erin feel suddenly weepy. "Thank you."

Julie squared her shoulders. "So, what are you going to do?"

"What do you mean?"

"You're still hot for him, right?"

Erin took another drink instead of answering.

"Oh, come on, it's just us, you're allowed to say it."

Erin cringed for a second. Then she lifted her chin. "Okay, yes, I'm hot for him. And I don't get hot for that many men."

"Don't I know it."

"What?"

"You work too hard," said Julie. "You don't date enough. But that's a whole other conversation. What are you going to do about Striker?"

Erin shrugged. "What can I do?" Lust after him

from afar? That was pretty pathetic. Thank goodness he was only staying one more day. After that, she should be able to handle Allan on her own.

"Turn the tables," said Julie.

Erin blinked blankly.

Julie grinned and rocked her head from side to side. "*You* massage *him* next time."

"I don't think there'll be a next time."

"I'm speaking metaphorically. Seduce him right back."

"You don't think that's a little—"

"Forward? Come on. This is the twenty-first century. Women are allowed to have sex drives."

"I was going to say risky. What if he really doesn't want me?"

Julie held up her glass and peered at Erin. "Erin, you do this right, he'll want you *bad* before he even knows what hit him."

STRIKER LAY on his back in the predawn darkness, watching as the glowing, green alarm clock numbers clicked over to six o'clock. What was he *thinking*, trying to seduce Erin like that?

This wasn't some cocktail party where she'd be expecting meaningless come-ons. This was her business trip. She'd hired him to *help* her, not to make callus, calculated advances.

He tipped his head back on the pillow, throwing one arm across his eyes, cringing as he replayed his little seduction scene for the thousandth time. He'd smiled *so* sincerely, spoken *so* intimately, found one excuse after another to touch her, worked his way under her clothes...

He cringed again. He couldn't go around sleeping with every woman he found sexy.

As soon as that thought was complete, his mind flicked to the past, where he'd done just that.

He'd called them dates.

His father had called them flings.

And for the first time in his life, Striker wondered which one of them was right. As the chill of that realization washed through him, the telephone at his bedside rang sharply in his ear.

He jolted upright, scrubbing one hand across his face, grabbing for the receiver. "Reeves here."

"Would you *please* explain to me what in the hell you're doing on Blue Earth Island?"

"Derek?"

"Yes. Derek. Remember me? Your big brother? The guy who's back here cleaning up your mess."

Striker gave his head a shake, trying to switch gears. "What mess?"

"You didn't think Mom would be upset after that little scene?"

Striker's mind slowly started to fire on all four cylinders. "How did you know I was here?"

"Our little brother's a private eye, remember? You can run, but you can't hide."

"I didn't run *or* hide. I flew a charter."

"Well, Mom thinks you're quitting."

"I'm not quitting."

"That's good."

"Is that what you wanted to know?"

"What I want to know is why you would bait him like that." There was no question that Derek was referring to their father.

"I'm not baiting anyone," said Striker.

There was the sound of running water behind Derek's voice. "One-night stands make him crazy."

"It was a date, not a one-night stand." Was it Striker's imagination, or did that answer sound a little too defensive?

Derek made a sharp sound of disbelief deep in his throat.

Striker regrouped. "When's the last time *you* got the entire family's permission to go out on a date?"

Whether Striker was feeling guilty or not, his brother was way out of line. Striker's personal life was none of Derek's or their father's business. Derek might be the golden child and the heir apparent, but that didn't give him the right to judge Striker.

Derek's voice turned smooth and confident. "On dates you generally know the woman's last name," he said. "And the first one traditionally ends with a kiss, it doesn't start in a hotel room."

"*You're* getting moralistic on me?"

Derek was no choirboy.

"I've sat back up till now," he said. "Because, quite frankly, I thought you'd grow out of it."

*Grow out of it?* "When did you become Dad's clone?"

A coffeemaker gurgled and dishes clattered in the background. "Look around you, Striker," said Derek. "Are you proud of your life?"

Striker wasn't about to answer that question. He might not be proud at this exact moment. But that didn't mean he needed his brother riding his ass.

"I'm old enough to make my own decisions," he said.

"Some of them didn't even speak English," said Derek.

Striker's shoulders stiffened. "I think you'd better back off now."

"And I think you'd better take a long, hard look at where you're going."

He did, did he? Well, Striker didn't think so. Instead of taking a long, hard look at his life, he took a long, hard look at the telephone receiver. Then he firmly hung it up.

He raked his hands through his hair.

The desire to quit Reeves-DuCarter and put some distance between himself and his family loomed in his mind again.

He didn't see how he had any choice.

It was bad enough fighting his father, but if he had to take on Derek, too…

He squeezed his eyes shut as the soul-searching from his long night settled into place.

Trouble was, even if he did quit his job and disowned his family, he'd still have to work through his feelings for Erin. He'd still have to battle this nagging guilt about all those other women. Whether Derek was around to judge him or not, he'd still have to change something.

He swore out loud.

He picked up the phone and dialed.

"Hello?" Derek answered.

"I'm sorry," said Striker.

There was a moment of shocked silence. "You're *what?*"

Clearly Derek was expecting the usual aftermath to one of their arguments. A couple of days of silence followed by the pretense that it had never happened.

"You heard me," said Striker. He wasn't about to repeat himself.

Derek didn't say a word—probably too stunned.

Striker stood up and paced across the room, phone to his ear. "It's not like they were quivering virgins, you know."

"You disillusion me."

Striker pressed the end of his fist against the cool windowpane. "They were old enough to make their own decisions. They knew the score. Most of them propositioned *me.*"

Okay, so that was after they learned about the jet

or after they took a ride in the Mustang. Striker felt his stomach tense up. He saw Erin's face again, so open, so trusting, so incredibly gorgeous. And what had he done with that?

"Not that I want to look a gift horse in the mouth, bro," said Derek. "But are you okay?"

"No," Striker answered honestly.

"What's going on?"

What was going on? A thousand things were rocking Striker's world. He had no idea where to start. "Last night," he said. "I started wondering what would happen if we had a sister."

Derek's reaction was slow and searching. "A *sister?*"

Striker had also wondered if he should get a girl-friend. Maybe that was his problem.

Nothing too serious. He didn't want somebody making unreasonable demands on his time. His job still required quite a bit of freedom and flexibility.

But it might be nice to get to know a woman on the inside as well as the outside—get to know her opinions and views. They could talk about world events, take long walks on the beach, curl up in front of his fireplace and sip wine together.

Striker suddenly realized the woman in his vision was Erin, and swore silently.

"Striker?" prompted Derek.

"Huh?"

"A sister?"

"Yeah." He pushed Erin to the back of his mind

and tapped his hand against the window. "Think about it for a minute. If we had a sister and some guy did to her what I've done to dozens of women, wouldn't we hunt him down and kill him?"

"I suppose that all depends on what you did to those women. Should we be talking to a lawyer about this?"

Striker dropped his hand by his side, sighing out loud in exasperation. He was trying to have a serious conversation here. "No. We shouldn't be talking to a lawyer."

"Had to ask. I mean you are a director of Reeves-DuCarter."

Trust Derek to keep the corporate interest at heart.

"I'm not talking about breaking the law. I'm talking about having been so cavalier about sex," said Striker.

"You're admitting that you're cavalier about sex?"

"Yeah."

"Why?"

"No reason," muttered Striker.

"What happened?"

Striker had no intention of going into specifics. "I've just been—"

"Is it a woman?"

"It's lots of women."

"No dice, little brother. What's her name?"

"There is no her."

Derek scoffed. "You think I'm stupid?"

"Erin. Okay. It's Erin."

The tone of Derek's voice changed completely. "Ahh."

"No, not *ahh*. See, I knew you'd think that. I've never even slept with her."

"Really?"

"We *just* met." As soon as the words were out, Striker realized how ridiculous they sounded coming from him, in that tone, in the middle of this conversation.

"But you're attracted to her," Derek guessed.

"Any guy would be attracted to her. She's gorgeous."

"Somebody finally say *no* to you?" Derek sounded disgustingly elated.

Striker squinted at the town of Pelican Cove, still and silent in the early morning. He took a deep breath. "*Erin* didn't say no."

"But I thought you—"

"I said no."

"You…"

"Surprised?"

"I'm checking the basement for pods."

"Cute."

"Hey, it's like you're Striker, only with morals."

"And ethics."

There was another clatter of dishes in the background. "You think you'll be able to hold out?"

"What are you talking about?"

"If this Erin likes you, and you're attracted to her,

and you don't want to sleep with her, you'd better get away from her. I mean, really, Striker, you know what you're like."

Yeah. Striker knew what he was like. "I can't leave."

"Why not?"

"I've got this dinner thing with her and her friend Julie and Allan Baldwin tonight."

"You're going to *date* her? Don't you think that's taking a big—"

"It's not a date. It's just dinner. They're from a jewelry company and they want Allan's diamonds, but Allan doesn't know that yet, and I'm—"

"You're setting Allan up?"

"No. I'm not setting Allan up. They're legit."

"Then at least stay away from her until the dinner."

"We're staying in the same beach house."

"I'm trying to help you reform here. But you don't make this easy, bro."

"I know." Easy was the last word Striker would use in this situation.

"So, what's she like?" asked Derek.

Striker thought about that one. Bossy? No, he didn't want to tell Derek that. Sexy? That went without saying. Determined? Organized? Funny? Vulnerable?

"Striker?"

"She's…complicated."

"Oh, well, that clarifies things for me." A blender roared and Derek raised his voice. "You know, I'm thinking you need to talk to Tyler."

"Tyler?" Striker couldn't imagine what his younger brother could add. "Why?"

"Because Tyler's already dealt with a complicated woman."

"Who?"

"Jenna."

Striker staggered back at the mention of his brother's new wife. "Don't be absurd."

He'd barely even met Erin. She was a problem, sure. But she wasn't *that* kind of problem.

The blender went silent. "Think about it, Striker. You could be falling for—"

"There's *nothing* to think about. Thanks so much for your advice, Derek. Maybe next time I *will* call Tyler."

Derek chuckled as Striker hung up the phone.

Falling for Erin.

Huh.

He was simply reordering his life. Nothing wrong with that. Maybe she did have a little bit to do with his shifting priorities. But not in any fundamental way.

He liked her, sure. He respected her, yeah. But his biggest problem was the physical attraction. Nothing new in that. He was physically attracted to women all the time.

Still, it was probably prudent to stay away for a while. He yanked open one of the bags from the Garment Barn and pulled out a pair of shorts and a T-shirt. No sense wallowing in temptation.

He'd take a jog down the beach and find something to occupy himself for the next couple or maybe *twelve* hours.

# 8

When Erin woke up, her headache was back. It could have been her despondency over Striker's rejection. Or, she had to admit, it might have been the brandy.

There was a light knock on her bedroom door.

She pulled the covers up over her chest and struggled into a sitting position in case it was Striker. She combed her fingers through her tangled hair and ran her tongue around the inside of her sticky mouth. She sure hoped it wasn't Striker.

"Yes?" she called

"It's Julie," Julie's voice floated through the door. "You alone?"

"Yeah. And I've got coffee."

"Come in. *Please*." Erin crossed her legs under the covers, trying to rub the shaft of pain out of her temples.

Julie pushed open the door, transferred one of the cups of coffee into the other hand, then closed the door with her hip.

The aroma of fresh-brewed coffee hit Erin like a

wall of sensation and suddenly the pain didn't seem quite so bad.

"Will you marry me?" she asked as Julie handed her the hot cup.

"You bet." Julie sat down on the end of the bed, twisting so that one leg was folded beneath her and she could face Erin. "Well, only if Allan says no."

Erin took a grateful sip, feeling better already. "You mean I can't beat out a hunky guy who owns a diamond mine?"

"Afraid not." Julie took a sip of her own coffee. "How're you holding up?"

Erin shrugged. "My ego's a little flattened, and I'm pretty sure I have a hangover, but it's a brand-new day." She winced at her own forced cheer.

"Good. Glad to hear you've got lots of energy for phase one."

Erin sighed as the caffeine hit her bloodstream. "Phase one of what?"

"You know, the part where you knock Striker's socks off…along with anything else he might be wearing at the time."

"Did I agree to this?"

Julie nodded. "Sure did. Along about 3:00 a.m."

"I must have been drunk."

"Nope. You were thinking perfectly clearly."

"Then why can't I remember?"

"Denial."

"Then how come I *can* remember the humiliating part?"

Julie shook her head. "I don't know what went wrong there. But he wants you. I can guarantee it. And you want him. And you're both consenting adults."

"You mean one of us is a consenting adult."

"He'll weaken. We'll weaken him."

Erin wasn't so sure she wanted to put her ego out there again. Sure, Striker was a gorgeous, sexy guy, but if he didn't want her, he didn't want her. "Explain to me why I should even try?"

Julie gave her a secretive smile. "Because it'll be totally worth it."

Erin grinned in return. "You are so bad."

"That's why you love me. I talk you into doing the things you really want to do anyway."

Erin paused to run that statement around in her brain.

Julie leaned forward, tapping herself on the chest. "I'm your wayward alter ego." Then she sat back. "Hey, maybe you're schizophrenic and I don't even exist."

"Then who made the coffee?"

"See. That's why you're the rational one. Now. Back to what we do to get Striker's attention. I *know* you can do sexy."

Erin glanced at the gray lingerie store package she'd dropped into one of the chairs. She hadn't had the guts to open it yet, but now she was curious. What did Striker think was sexy?

She set her coffee cup down on the bedside table, slipped out from under the covers and crossed the room.

"What's that?" asked Julie, turning to watch her progress.

Erin shook her head. "I don't know. Striker gave it to me."

"When?"

"When we went clothes shopping. He came up with some crazy idea that if I was dressing him, it was only fair that he dress me."

"And you agreed to that?" Julie sounded surprised.

"It wasn't like I had a lot of choice. You saw how he looked when we first got here. Besides, I had no intention of living up to my end of the deal."

"You lied to him to get him to wear a suit?"

"That's right."

Julie stood up. "Go, Erin. Let's see it."

Erin opened the bag and pulled out some silky cloth wrapped in mauve tissue paper. There was a little gold seal holding the tissue paper closed.

"Classy," said Julie.

"Don't be too hasty. Striker picked it out himself." Erin ripped open the seal.

Something made of apricot satin slithered onto the table. Julie picked up a camisole top. It had spaghetti straps and was trimmed with flat, apricot lace at the neck and hemline.

Erin picked up the matching shorts. They were

whisper thin, with a soft elastic waist and matching lace insets at the outsides of the thighs.

"Gorgeous," Julie breathed.

Erin was stunned. The outfit was sexy, sure. But it was also classically beautiful. No whalebone stays, or peekaboo nipples or black laced garters.

How had Striker come up with something like this?

"Let him get a gander at you in this," said Julie. "And you're halfway home."

"I couldn't," said Erin. Though she was past the point of denying she wanted to seduce Striker. Maybe Julie was her wayward alter ego.

Julie held the camisole up to her chest. "I don't mean parade in front of him like a stripper. Make it look like an accident. It'll drive him crazy."

"He's already accidentally seen me in my underwear, and it was darned good underwear, too."

Julie chuckled deeply. "Yeah, but he never bought you that underwear. This is *his* underwear. Trust me, phase two is definitely letting him see you in this."

The phone rang.

As she crossed the room to answer it, Erin had to admit, she got a little shiver at the thought of Striker seeing her in the camisole and shorts.

She picked up the receiver. "Hello?"

"Erin?"

"Yes."

"It's Allan."

Erin felt her eyes go wide at the unexpected announcement. "Good morning, Allan."

"I was wondering if Julie was up yet?" he asked.

"Sure. She's right here. Just a minute." She covered the mouthpiece of the phone. "He wants to talk to *you*."

Julie grinned and gave Erin a high five on the way past. "All right, partner."

Erin sat down on the bed to listen to Julie's side of the conversation, reminding herself that her energy should be focused on Allan not Striker.

Forget the sexy underwear, they had dinner to cook.

"Hello?" said Julie.

Then she smiled. "Just fine."

She winked at Erin. "Me, too."

Erin folded the silk apricot shorts and placed them back on the tissue paper. She felt another little thrill at the thought of Striker's hands on the soft fabric. She quickly tamped it down. Allan was the man who counted today.

"Of course," said Julie. "We're not busy this morning. Happy to help."

Erin felt a smile grow on her face. It sounded like Allan wanted to see them again, even before tonight. This was fantastic.

"An hour's fine," said Julie.

Erin folded the camisole. They'd have to shower and have a quick breakfast, but there was nothing stopping them from a visit with Allan this morning.

"Sure. See you then." Julie hung up the phone.

"What?" asked Erin.

"He's offered to bring the wine tonight."

"That's very nice of him."

"Isn't it? I think he's a genuinely nice person. Even with all that money." Julie frowned.

"What?" asked Erin.

"I have to tell you, I'm starting to feel guilty about lying to him."

That surprised Erin. "You? My wayward alter ego? The one who once told a man she was moving to Paris?"

"Hey, this is business, not dating."

"And we're not lying to him. We're simply postponing the truth."

Julie looked unconvinced. "It doesn't feel right."

"We'll tell him tonight," Erin promised.

"For sure?"

"Yes."

"Okay."

"So, does he want to see us about something?" asked Erin.

"Uh…" Julie turned and straightened the quilt on Erin's bed. "Just me," she said to the wall.

Erin felt a shaft of disappointment. "Just you?"

Julie turned back. "He asked if I'd come and help pick out the wine." She paused. "You mind?"

Erin forced herself to smile. She'd still get to see Allan later tonight, and Julie seeing him again so soon could only help to strengthen the relationship.

"Of course I don't mind. You soften up Allan, and I'll stay here and work on Striker."

Erin glanced at the apricot outfit, making up her mind. Looked like she did have some time free this morning, and she had promised to wear it for him. She could be subtle, find a way to protect her dignity if he wasn't interested.

"Striker left," said Julie.

Erin's stomach shifted. "He did?"

"I think it was around seven."

"Oh." That wasn't disappointment she felt. She had a hundred things to do today. She had to go to the bakery, pick up some new candles, stop at the market... Julie had her job to take care of today and Erin had her own. Striker was less than a footnote in the operation.

She stuffed the silk back into the gray bag.

STRIKER MADE IT about ten miles before he realized he hadn't thought this through. He was thirsty and sweaty, and he was dying for a shower. But all he had was the five dollar bill he'd stuffed in the pocket of his shorts.

If he'd brought along his credit cards, he could have rented a hotel room, picked up some new clothes and freshened up for the day.

As it was, he had a choice of staying sweaty and hungry or going back to the beach house to face Erin. Though sweat wasn't his first choice, facing Erin after last night was definitely his last.

She probably wasn't even speaking to him this morning. Maybe she never would again.

His father would get a kick out of the irony.

Striker slowed to a walk on the loose sand, gazing at the beachfront houses. They were smaller at this end of the island, still nice, but not as sprawling and palatial as they were down near Allan's place.

He came to an access path and decided to walk into the business section of town and buy a bottle of water. At least he had enough money to stave off dehydration while he waited out the day. After dinner, he'd rent his own hotel room. Then he'd take off at first light and try to patch up his life. Maybe he could back off on the overseas women and meet his father halfway.

If there was any justice in the world, Erin would sign a contract with Allan and forget she ever met a man named Striker.

He sat down on a bench at the head of the path and removed his running shoes. Then he dumped the sand out, shook his socks and put everything back on again. There, that felt a little bit better. He could last the day.

It was about six blocks up to Main Street and by the time he got there, his wet shirt had cooled in the wind. Businesses were beginning to open. Traffic was light, since it was barely nine o'clock and this was predominately a vacation town.

He could see a small grocery store about half a

block down Main Street. As he headed toward it, a flash of bright red caught his attention. He turned to look, then stopped and stared in awe into the open door of an oversized garage set next to a modest house, among towering cedar trees.

He took a couple of steps closer, his thirst forgotten.

It couldn't be...

He waited for a blue sedan to make it past him, and he trotted across the street.

There, he stopped. He wasn't crazy.

An immaculate, BA Swallow airplane was parked in the garage, its silver wings nearly touching each wall.

Striker walked toward it. As far as he knew, there were only two of them left flying in the world.

At the edge of the open bay doorway he could see a gray-haired man working at the bench, bent over the engine block, fitting pistons.

"Hello?" Striker called out.

The man turned. He was tall and robust looking, although he must have been in his late fifties. He had a thick, gray mustache and dark eyebrows over pale blue eyes. "Hi, there," he greeted.

"Great plane," said Striker.

The man smiled. Wiping his hands on a rag, he took a few steps toward the fuselage, looking up at the Swallow with an appreciative smile. "She's a beauty all right."

"Yours?" asked Striker.

"Belongs to my sons and I," said the man. He moved toward Striker and stuck out his hand. "Roger Cameron."

Striker shook his hand. "Striker Reeves. You owned her for long?"

"Coming up on twenty years," said Roger. "You're welcome to come in and have a look."

Striker gladly accepted the invitation to take a closer look at the magnificent plane. It had obviously been lovingly restored. He ran his fingertips along the leading edge of the wing. "She fly?"

"Hope she will soon," said Roger. "Airframe's all done. I just have to finish rebuilding the engine."

Striker nodded to the bench. "Did you have to go with oversized pistons?"

"Slightly," said Roger. "Honed out the cylinders. Going two-thou."

"Best way," said Striker. "I've got a little Tiger Moth and a Thunderjet myself. Love to get them up in the air someday."

"You're a pilot?" asked Roger.

Striker nodded. "And a mechanic when I have the time." He nodded to the engine block. "You want a hand?"

Roger smiled, revealing slightly crooked teeth. "You sure you want to get your clothes dirty?"

"Can't think of anything I'd rather do than put a little elbow grease into this baby. Guess I must be missing my two back home."

"On vacation?" asked Roger.

"Visiting a friend," said Striker.

"To be perfectly honest with you, I'd love a hand. It's been a few years since any of my boys had time to come by and help."

"They move off the island?"

Roger nodded. "My oldest opened up a fancy law firm in New York—his mom's real proud."

"How many sons do you have?" asked Striker.

"Two. Younger one…" Roger returned to the bench, and Striker followed. "Younger one is tending bar in a Las Vegas casino."

"Either of them fly?" asked Striker, picking up a micrometer to check the piston measurements.

They fell into an easy conversation as they fitted the pistons and rings, and the morning flew by quickly.

They took a break at noon for sandwiches and iced tea with Roger's wife.

Afterward, Roger got out the connecting rods.

"She has the patience of a saint," he said as the door closed behind his wife. "I've spent a fortune on this plane and she's never complained, not once in twenty years."

"In this condition," said Striker, admiring the Swallow once again, "it has to be *worth* a fortune."

Roger got a faraway look in his eyes. "I've often thought that if I sold it, I could take her on a world cruise. I know she's always wanted to travel. But, then I think maybe I'll end up with a grandchild who's interested in flying, and I'd regret selling her."

"It's tough when your sons have different ambitions than you," Striker observed, thinking of the tension between himself and his father.

Roger shook his head. "Don't get me wrong, I'd never want them to take up flying to please me. Everyone has to find his own path in life. And things are working out very well for Adam."

"But Ben?" Striker prompted. In their stories, Ben had been the headstrong child.

"Ah, Ben," said Roger with a smile and a shake of his head. "We're a little worried about that boy."

"How so?" asked Striker, helping himself to Roger's toolbox and plunging on the connecting rods.

"Molly and I met in Vegas," said Roger.

That surprised Striker. They both seemed so down-to-earth and settled. He'd pictured them both growing up in the Midwest. "You're kidding?"

"I was a dealer," said Roger. "Fast money, fast everything. Molly was in one of the shows. She was gorgeous back then. Still is, of course."

"Definitely," said Striker, trying to picture a younger Molly on stage in feathers and sequins.

"I think she saved me from a life of decadence and debauchery."

"I find that very hard to imagine," said Striker.

Roger laughed to himself. "Here's the secret. You remember this. It's not your kids taking a different path that worries you. It's when you see them making the same mistakes that you panic."

"Ben's on the road to decadence and debauchery?"

Roger winked at Striker. "I'm sure he's having a wonderful time."

By the time dusk settled, they'd finished hooking up the connecting rods and torqued the cylinders.

Molly appeared once again to invite Striker for dinner.

At the mention of the word dinner, Striker's stomach plummeted. He glanced at his watch and realized Allan was due to arrive in less than an hour.

He quickly thanked Molly and Roger for their hospitality and promised to stop in before he left in the morning. Then he took off at a fast jog, taking the shortcut through town.

# 9

ERIN WAS TRYING not to panic as she stared at the plump, sockeye salmon lying on the countertop. Allan was due in fifteen minutes and she had all the ingredients for Striker's salmon in dill sauce, but no recipe and no Striker.

She'd gone from feeling slighted to worried to annoyed. If he was going to leave her high and dry, the least he could have done was warn her.

So he wasn't attracted to her. Fine. He'd told her as much last night. He'd also promised to stay for the dinner. It wasn't like she was going to leap out from the hallway and attack him.

Okay, so maybe she had been planning to give him a glimpse of the apricot silk camisole. But *he* was the one who'd bought it for her. In fact, he was the one who'd started flirting in the first place.

She sure hadn't pulled *him* down into *her* lap to plant a kiss. And she sure hadn't massaged every square inch of *his* skin. It wasn't fair for him to hold it against her because she responded to his sensuality.

She heard the front door open and close, and her

stomach clenched, first with relief and then with annoyance. She marched into the living room to see a
sweat-drenched Striker standing in the foyer in
shorts and a T-shirt. He was covered in grease from
head to toe.

Julie was staring at him in wide-eyed silence.

"Allan will be here in *fifteen minutes*." Erin's voice
was strident as she headed for the staircase. She really felt like grabbing Striker by the ear and hauling
him up to his room. "Where have you *been*?"

"I got delayed," said Striker, breathing deeply,
one hand on his side. His hair was damp across his
forehead. He looked even worse than the day they'd
met him.

She couldn't even imagine where he'd found so
much grease and oil on this island. She mounted the
stairs, motioning for him to follow her. "Come *on*. We
have to get you dressed. Julie, will you entertain
Allan?"

"No problem," said Julie.

"Right behind you," said Striker on a gasp.

Erin trotted up the stairs, pushing open his bedroom door, heading straight for the en suite bathroom. "Wear the gray suit. I pressed your other shirt,
and the tie's hanging on a hook on the inside of the
door." She opened the glass door of the corner
shower stall and cranked the taps.

"You have exactly five minutes to shower. Then I
want you to shave, blow dry your hair and get down

to the kitchen." As she spoke, her frustration grew. Hadn't he understood how important this was? "I don't understand how you could be so irresponsible."

"That's enough, Erin." His tone was cold. "I just busted my ass to get here and help you out."

Erin whirled to find him leaning against the doorjamb, arms crossed over his chest. She raised her voice above the sound of the spray. "Then why are you two hours late?"

"And I don't do well with orders."

She took a step toward him, regretting the moment she'd decided he could help her. "And I'd rather not have to give them. But when you're in my employ and you show up hours late, covered in dirt and grime, having given no thought to how your behavior will affect anybody else but yourself, you can damn well learn to take orders."

The steam from the running shower began to billow out into the room.

"Your *employ*?"

"I *am* paying you."

"Not anymore you're not."

"What's that supposed to mean?"

"I quit."

Erin's frustration flipped to panic. "You can't quit now."

"I'm not quitting now."

Thank goodness. She moved away from the shower door, intending to brush past him into the bedroom and give him his privacy. Plus, she needed to get out of all this steam before she wilted. "Then I'll just leave you to—"

"I'm quitting retroactively."

Erin stopped, a short pace away from him. "You're what?"

"This was a bad idea from the start, Erin. I shouldn't be here. And you don't need me."

Didn't need him? Sure she needed him. There was Allan, the salmon...

"I'll pay you for the clothes and my share of the beach house," said Striker. "I can get my own hotel room tonight and fly out in the morning."

Erin swallowed. She didn't want Striker out of her life this second. Sure, he was frustrating and coarse and constantly getting dirty. And he didn't respond well to direction. But, he was cooking tonight. And now that it came down to it, she was still debating the merits of modeling the apricot outfit.

Maybe she'd have chickened out in the end. But, maybe...

"Don't look at me like that," he growled.

"Like what?"

"Erin, we have got to get away from each other."

Not yet. He couldn't leave yet. Erin wasn't ready. "You're going to abandon me before we get the contract? Before you cook the salmon? Before I wear your outfit?"

Okay, that last bit was bold. Alter ego Julie would be proud.

Striker's eyes darkened at the word *outfit*, and he took a step forward, pinning her with his sexy, midnight blue eyes. "*Especially* before I..." He took a single, deep breath. "...cook the salmon."

She blinked.

He'd made a joke.

In the middle of *this*, he'd made a joke? Maybe all wasn't lost.

"It fits perfectly," she said, daring to lean in closer.

"The salmon?"

She smiled. "The camisole. You should see me in it."

"No. I shouldn't."

For a second there, she thought she'd misjudged him again. She searched his expression. "Why?"

"I'm scared."

"Of what?"

"Me."

Okay, she was going for broke here. She moved in even closer, letting her eyes go bedroom soft. "Well, I'm not scared of you."

Striker drew in another breath as clouds of steam billowed around them. "You should be."

"Why?"

"Because I'm a corrupt person."

She could feel the smile grow on her face. "What makes you think I have the slightest interest in your ethics?"

Striker didn't say a word.

She boldly reached up and touched his unshaven face. "I'm after your body, Striker, not your soul."

The doorbell sounded.

"You sure about that?" he asked.

"Positive."

Then Striker peeled off his sweaty T-shirt.

He was getting in the shower. He wasn't leaving. Erin's heart gave a little leap of joy.

"Take off your dress," he said.

A sexual thrill zipped through her. "Now?"

"I don't shower unless you shower with me."

"Another ultimatum?"

"Take it or leave it."

Erin took it.

She was probably crazy, and she'd probably live to regret this. But at the moment, she just hoped Julie would keep Allan entertained.

She turned around and lifted her hair, so that Striker could unzip her dress.

The zipper rasped softly in her ear as his rough fingertips trailed down the skin of her back.

His hands pushed the straps of her black dress off her shoulders and Erin shivered.

"I'm sorry," he whispered as his warm lips touched the curved of her neck.

"For what?" she breathed, closing her eyes as his tongue touched her flesh.

"Everything I've ever done and everything I ever will do to hurt you."

His sentiment was sweet but totally unnecessary. She smiled. "You're not hurting me now."

He pushed her dress down farther and it slithered to the bathroom floor. "I'm not a nice guy."

She turned in his arms. "So you've said."

His hand closed over her breast. "I'm just trying to warn you."

Sparks of desire shot through her chest and she tipped her head up for a kiss. "I've been warned."

"Just so we're clear," he whispered as his mouth closed in.

"We're clear."

Their lips met and a satisfying wave of passion arced through Erin's body. She wrapped her arms around his neck, opening her mouth, absorbing the hot, sweet taste of Striker.

He reached behind himself, pushed the bathroom door closed and flipped the lock. Then he pushed off his shorts and her panties and lifted her against him.

Heat shot through the center of her being. She kissed her way along his salty shoulder, burying her face in his neck and inhaling deeply.

He captured her mouth once more, holding her tight, crossing the small room, and turning them both to bring her buttocks to rest on the countertop. It was a cool, smooth counterpoint to the rough heat of

Striker's skin. The shower spray splattered noisily against the glass, and the steam billowed around them, releasing the scents of citrus and wild flowers.

He pulled back slightly, his breath puffing against her face. "Erin?"

She slowly opened her eyes. Her vision was blurry and the room was a haze.

His hand cupped her chin and he held her gaze. "I swear, this has never happened before." His deep voice tripped along her nervous system.

"You're a great liar." She smiled as she leaned forward and kissed him deeply. "Keep it up."

"But—"

"Shh." She touched her finger to his lips. "You don't have to confess to me."

He drew the finger into his mouth.

A pulse throbbed up her arm as his tongue swirled around her knuckle. "You don't have to lie to me," she whispered.

The pulse grew in strength and moved out to engulf her body. "You don't…have…to…"

He drew her finger out, pausing with his lips against the moist tip. "What do you want me to do?"

Erin's heartbeat deepened. She wasn't particularly bold when it came to sex. But as she stared into Striker's eyes she knew they'd gone past the point of being shy.

She took his hand and placed it on her breast.

He brushed his thumb across one nipple. She

moaned and closed her eyes, dropping her head back, pointing to her exposed neck.

He kissed her there, his thumb brushing back and forth, raising goose bumps, making her skin itch in every intimate place.

"What else?" he asked against her neck.

Emboldened by the desire oozing out of her very pores, she took his other hand and slowly tucked it between their bodies.

His breathing rasped in her ear as he touched her heat. He stroked her, stretched her, entered her. He knew exactly what he was doing, and she didn't even care why.

She thought about asking him what he wanted.

She didn't know if she dared.

Then she realized it was all or nothing. This magical moment would never come again.

She held up her empty palms, wriggling her fingers. "What about you?"

He grinned against her skin. "Touch me."

"Where?"

"Anywhere."

She slowly shook her head. "You don't tell me, I don't touch."

He moved his hand in a way that made her squirm and moan at the same time.

"Ultimatums, Erin?"

"Payback time."

He chuckled low. "Okay." He leaned into her ear,

whispered in graphic terms just where and how and with which part of her body he wanted to be touched. Then he gave more detail. Then he told her how it would make him feel.

Her body nearly melted into him.

"Now," she whispered hoarsely. "Right...now."

He slipped his hand from between them, barely pausing for the condom, and then he was inside her, telling her over and over again how he loved her touch and how wonderful she made him feel.

The steam drenched their bodies. It nearly obliterated the light.

Condensation clung to every surface. And when Erin reached out to grasp something her hand slid down the glass shower door. She managed to grab a towel with the other hand and yanked it from the hanger.

Striker moved faster and harder within her, taking her higher and higher, until she thought she might scream from sheer sensation.

She clenched her jaw, her breath rasping against his ear, holding back the emotion that wanted to escape.

"Let it out," he said.

She shook her head.

"Yes."

"Julie...Allan..."

"Won't hear you."

She shook her head, and he took her higher.

She grasped his shoulders, digging her fingernails harder and harder into his skin.

"Do it," he groaned.

She couldn't. She wasn't a screamer.

"You are so beautiful," he whispered in her ear. "You feel like satin, wet satin." His hand slipped between their bodies.

He touched her, and she nearly came off the countertop.

She groaned in his ear.

"That's it," he whispered. His fingertip shifted and she gasped his name.

"Let it out, sweetheart."

She was going to scream. It was building inside her and there was nowhere for it to go.

He thrust inside. He stroked outside. He whispered outrageous compliments and sexy words of encouragement.

And, suddenly it was there, a loud, high involuntary sound that echoed inside her brain as her body convulsed and the world collapsed around her.

He said her name over and over again, squeezing her tight, kissing her cheeks, her temple, her eyelids.

After long minutes of aftershocks, he smoothed her hair back from her forehead. "You okay?"

She tried to get some words to form in what had become the jumble of her brain. She finally gave up and simply nodded.

He held her close and rocked her back and forth.

"Erin, sweetheart. I'm not lying when I say I have *never* done that before."

STRIKER KNEW he should be feeling guilty. Or at least repentant. At the *very* least, he shouldn't be humming as he combed his damp hair and tightened his tie.

He'd failed miserably. He'd promised himself he wouldn't touch her, considered it a kind of test to prove he actually had a scrap of a moral code inside him.

Looked like he didn't.

Looked like he was irredeemable.

Looked like his father was right.

Too bad he couldn't stop grinning like an idiot.

He couldn't wait to see her again, even with Julie and Allan as chaperones. He wanted to watch her move, hear her talk, inhale her scent.

He quickly shrugged into his jacket and headed for the bedroom door. After their shower, Erin had crept back to her own room to fix her hair and makeup. He hoped she wouldn't take too long.

He trotted down the stairs to meet Allan and Julie.

They were locked in conversation on the couch. Judging by their absorption in each other's words, Striker doubted they'd even noticed how long Erin had been gone.

That was good.

He knew she was feeling self-conscious.

"Hey, Allan," Striker greeted.

Allan and Julie looked up, appearing startled. A slight blush rose in Julie's cheeks, making Striker wonder what they'd been talking about.

He smiled to himself. Well, well, well.

He gestured to the kitchen door. "I'm under orders to start the salmon. Anybody need a drink or anything?"

"We opened a bottle of the cabernet," said Allan, raising his glass. "Pour you one?"

"In a few minutes."

"You need any help in there?" asked Julie.

Striker shook his head. "Chef Striker works alone. You two just...*carry on*."

Allan's eyes twinkled.

Julie blushed.

So Striker *had* interrupted something. Interesting.

He headed for the kitchen, warmed up the grill and located a suitable saucepan.

Somebody had already made a salad, and there was fresh bread waiting in a covered basket. Erin had told him she planned to pick up a cake from the bakery, so it looked like the salmon was all he needed to worry about.

Just as well, considering it was his one and only specialty.

As he lay the salmon filets on the indoor grill, the door to the kitchen opened. Erin, Julie and Allan joined him.

"Erin didn't want you to get lonely," said Allan, pulling out a chair at the table for Julie.

Erin headed for Striker. "Can I do anything?" she asked in a loud voice, coming up close, peering into the pot he was stirring.

Then she whispered low, "Did they look suspicious? Did they say anything?"

"Relax," Striker whispered back. "They're ignoring us. I think they like each other."

Erin peeped over her shoulder to where Julie and Allan sat laughing at the table.

Erin's black dress hugged her gorgeous curves. Tendrils from her upswept hair curled around her face, barely brushing her smooth shoulders. And her dangling earrings made her look exotic and mysterious.

He couldn't summon up a single scrap of regret.

"You look stunning," Striker whispered in her ear.

"Shh," said Erin.

"It's not a secret. They can see it, too."

She elbowed him in the ribs.

He loved having her near, love savoring the memories. He wanted to put his arm around her, kiss her temple, inhale her scent, whisper silly words.

"Erin..." He could hear the longing in his own voice.

"Striker..." Her tone was warning.

"I want you again."

"Don't."

"I can't help it."

"I mean don't talk about it. Not right now."

His chest tightened. "When?"

"Later."

"Really?"

She looked up at him, a promise shining in her chocolate eyes. "Later."

Striker nearly dropped a salmon filet as he tried to flip it over.

Silence suddenly descended into the room.

"I'll pour you a glass then," she said in a normal tone.

"Great," said Striker, picking up a spoon to stir the sauce. *Great, great, great!*

She moved away to get another wineglass from the cupboard.

As the sauce smoothed and thickened, Striker pulled the fish platter out of the oven where it had been warming. "It's almost ready," he announced.

"Table's already set in the dining room," said Erin.

Everyone pitched in, picking up wine bottles and dishes of food, while Striker arranged the fish on the platter. Then they all trooped into the dining room.

Dinner went smoothly, with conversational topics ranging from politics to movies.

As they finished the chocolate torte, Erin stood up from her chair. "I almost forgot, Allan. I thought you might be interested in this."

She picked up a catalogue from the side table and set it in front of him. Her voice sounded credibly casual as she spoke. "My boss gave it to me just before

I left New York. It's an advance copy of Elle's new designs for next year."

Striker stilled, nervous for Erin as he waited for Allan's reaction.

Allan looked down at the catalogue, then back up at Erin. He blinked. "You work for Elle?"

Erin nodded, keeping her expression neutral. "We both do. Didn't we mention that last night?"

Allan shook his head.

He glanced at Julie.

Julie focused on her torte.

"I thought we had," said Erin.

"I was sure they had," said Striker.

Allan shot him an incredulous look, clearly wondering why the hell Striker was lying.

Striker tried for a go-along-with-it stare.

Allan's eyes narrowed. Then he turned back to Erin. "Maybe you did mention it."

"I thought so," said Striker, grateful for Allan's tact, hoping he wouldn't hold anything against Erin and Julie.

"Why don't we clear up the dishes," said Julie, dropping her napkin into her half-finished dessert.

Looking relieved, Erin rose with her. "Take a look through the catalogue," she said to Allan. "You can take it home if you'd like."

The two women gathered up a handful of dessert dishes and headed for the kitchen.

Allan sat back, scooping his napkin from his lap

and dropping it on the table. "So, how long have you known they were setting me up?"

"Maybe it's just a coincidence," Striker suggested.

"Like hell. Two bombshells from Elle Jewelers show up with you? That means I'm a mark."

"They're not bombshells."

Allan arched his eyebrows.

"Well, I mean, of *course* they're bombshells. But Erin's a buyer and Julie's a gemologist. They're legit."

"What happened? Did they con you into this?"

"Not exactly."

"Are you in on a cut?"

"Of course I'm not in on a cut."

Allan tipped his chin up. "So, what've they got on you?"

A pair of gorgeous brown eyes. "It's a long story."

Allan gave a half grin. "One of your usual stories?"

"No. It's not that." Well, it was a little bit that. But Erin was different.

"I have to admit," said Allan. "They're a hell of an improvement over the last two guys Elle sent."

"You mean, all this time, a pretty woman was all they needed?"

Allan snorted. "Right. I'm having a hard time believing you went along with this."

Striker shrugged. "Hey, you're a big boy. You can take care of yourself." He grinned. "When's the last time you made a business decision based on your libido."

Allan took a sip of his wine. "Never." Then he smiled. "Of course, I have to admit, I am enjoying their attempt. Do me a favor. Don't tell them I'm onto them."

Striker hesitated. "Why? What are you going to do?"

Allan smiled. "Have another glass of wine and chat with two beautiful women."

"And the contract?"

Allan shrugged. "I'll evaluate it on its merits, just like every other contract I've ever been offered."

# 10

STRIKER'S TIME WAS running out. He was supposed to be at a Reeves-DuCarter shareholders meeting tomorrow, and Erin was on the verge of offering Allan the contract. No matter which way it went for her, their real lives were about to take over. She'd go back to New York and Striker would go back to Seattle.

He tried to curb his impatience as he waited for Julie to go to sleep so he could sneak down the hall to Erin and share their last hours together.

After the sounds in Julie's room went silent, he forced himself to wait another half hour.

But the minute his self-imposed time restriction was up, he headed for his bedroom door and crept down the hall.

He slowly opened Erin's door, not sure what to expect. She could be asleep. They hadn't made any concrete plans, he was just going on the vague, whispered *later* that had set his blood on fire.

The lights were dim and she was awake. She was standing next to the bed, lighting a small candle. She turned to look at him and blew out the match. The candlelight rose behind her, silhouetting her gorgeous body. She was wearing the lingerie he'd bought for her, and the sight made his mouth go dry.

He soundlessly shut the door.

The curtains billowed with the change in pressure. A window was partway open and the ocean breeze was up. Waves echoed on the sandy shore.

She looked like an angel in the candle's glow.

The outside world shut down as Striker made his way toward her. He wanted to pull her into his arms and make frantic love with her. *Now*, without wasting an extra second.

But he also wanted to pull her tight and hold on to her forever. He wanted to know her thoughts, her secrets, her hopes, her fears.

He slowed to a stop in front of her, tamping down his desire, gently reaching out to brush her fingertips with his own. Even that light touch sent sparks of desire shooting along his system.

"Hi," she breathed.

He loved her voice. He took the small step that brought his body against hers. "Hi."

He inhaled deeply, reveling in her scent, resisting an urge to bury his face in her neck. He had to take it slow this time.

He drew back, cupping her cheeks so that he could gaze at her beauty, tunneling his spread fingers into her hair and placing a tender kiss on her full lips. "I missed you," he whispered.

"It's only been an hour."

"I still missed you." He kissed her again. She tasted of sweet chocolate and dark passion. A man could lose his senses in a woman like her. But Striker was determined to make this night last. "I hope you're not tired."

She shook her head.

"That's good to hear. Because I'm not leaving you for a long, long time."

He stepped away to look at her, taking her hand to maintain their physical connection. He shook his head in wonder. "Man, I have good taste."

She grinned, smoothing one hand down the front of the camisole. "I agree."

"I meant in women," said Striker. "Though the outfit's not bad, either."

Her smile widened.

"I have a fantasy," he said, lifting her hand to kiss her palm.

Her delicate eyebrows rose, her expression turned to a mixture of trepidation and interest.

"Not *that* kind of a fantasy," he chuckled, kissing her fingertips one at a time. "Though I'm sure we can come up with something later."

He reached down and tugged the big comforter off her bed. He turned, leading her by the hand toward the balcony door. "Come on."

"It's cold out there," she protested.

"I'll keep you warm."

He slid the glass door open and they stepped through the threshold onto a breezy balcony overlooking the silver beach and the shifting, black ocean.

"Brrr," she shivered.

He sat down on a padded lounger and spread his legs, motioning for her to sit in between. "Trust me."

She sat, fitting her bottom between his thighs. He quickly covered them both with the comforter and wrapped his arms around her.

"See?" he whispered in her ear, reveling in the feel of her smooth curves.

"This is nice," she sighed.

The ocean breeze caressed their faces. The roar of the waves surrounded them. And a billion stars winked around the high, half moon.

Striker idly caressed her silk-covered stomach. He kissed the top of her head, breathing in the citrus scent that took him back to the day she'd washed his hair and that first mind-blowing kiss.

The second his lips had touched hers, his universe changed forever. She was his frame of reference now, the kisses by which he would judge all the rest. He should probably consider the implications of that.

But not right now.

Maybe later.

She softened against him, her bottom sinking deeper into the V of his legs. He tried to focus on something else, like the stars or the waves or the wind. They'd make amazing love before the night was over, but he wanted the buildup to take hours.

He was feeling a little guilty. Twenty hot minutes on the bathroom counter wasn't exactly his most stellar performance.

He tipped his head back, focusing on the sky.

"When I was a boy," he said. "My family used to take vacations at the beach. Derek, Tyler and I would sleep on the front porch. And the sky looked just like this one. Big, endless, full of mystery."

"I used to wish on the stars," she said.

"What did you wish for?"

"Money mostly. Even as a kid, I knew we were poor. But sometimes I'd wish for toys, new clothes, candy."

Striker's heart contracted and guilt crept in once again. He'd had a five-bedroom beach house, while she had wished for candy.

"Is there anything you want now?" he asked, vowing to get it for her if it was within his power.

There was a smile in her voice. "This week? For Allan to love my contract."

Okay, well, Striker would work on that one.

"For this moment? Nothing."

His arms contracted around her. "But we've got all these stars. It's a shame to let them go to waste."

"Then you come up with something," she said. "What would you wish for?"

"Right now?" That was easy. "For time to stop."

Erin sighed. "That would be nice."

"Look at that." He pointed to the sky.

"A shooting star. Do we wish on it?"

"We could. But I think it's a satellite."

Her body moved against him as she laughed. "Tell me another wish."

"What kind of wish?"

"Something important. What do you want out of life?"

"World peace."

"That's too easy. Smaller. Something for you?"

Striker thought about that. "Family peace."

"Yeah?"

"Mmm, hmm," he said.

"There are problems in your family?"

"I think there are problems in every family."

"Tell me about yours."

"That could take all night."

"Give me the highlights."

"Okay. My dad and I don't get along. It upsets my mother."

"Why?"

"She hates to see us fight."

Erin gave him a light elbow in the ribs. "Why don't you get along with your dad?"

"He wants me to do everything his way."

There was a smile in her tone. "Let me guess. And *you* want to do everything *your* way?"

"I compromise."

She nodded against his chest. "Sure you do... Mr. Ultimatum. Your poor father."

"If you'd ever met Jackson Reeves you wouldn't pity him."

"Striker, I've only known you three days and I feel sorry for anyone who has to go up against you."

"I let you change everything about me."

She tipped her head to look him in the eyes. "Let's keep this in perspective. You bought a suit."

"You cut my hair."

"Only because it needed it."

"My father is unbending and unreasonable."

"You ever try to look at anything from his perspective?"

"I don't have to. He does that all by himself."

Erin pulled one of his hands out from under the comforter. She kissed his knuckles. "You are a stubborn man."

"Then how come you always get everything all your way?"

She flipped over, balancing on her knees, leaning against his chest. "You think I get things *my* way?"

"All the time."

She smiled secretively and walked her fingers up his bare arm. "Why don't we just test that, hmm?"

The last thing Striker needed at the moment was a test that involved full-frontal Erin teasing him.

"Why don't you tell me about your family, instead?"

"You're not getting off that easy," she said.

"I told you about my dad. It's your turn."

"Are you going to get stubborn about this?"

"I'm not stubborn. Now tell me about your family."

She shrugged. "Okay. It was just me and my mom. She died the year I graduated high school."

"Oh, Erin. I'm sorry."

"It was ten years ago."

He kissed her forehead, suddenly wondering who in the world took care of Erin. Did she have close friends? Where did she spend Christmas? Who took care of her when she was sick?

He couldn't imagine life without his mother, his brothers, even his father.

He had a sudden urge to take Erin home and introduce her to everyone. Maybe his mother could fuss over her for a while. Maybe that would help.

Even as he wished for it, he knew it was impossible. This was a stolen moment out of each of their lives, and it was all they had. He focused in on the brightest star in the sky and wished that time would stop.

It didn't.

Striker knew it hadn't because the wind kept blowing, the tide kept rising, and Erin suddenly snapped up the armrests on the lounger, and they reclined with a jolt.

"Hey—"

"Hey, what?" She wriggled up his body until she was lying fully on top of him.

"What are you doing?"

Then she sat up and let the comforter slide off her shoulders. There was a gleam in her eyes. "Since you're so sure I always get things my own way..." she said and stripped off her camisole.

Striker sucked in a hard breath as he drank in the sight of her half-naked body glowing in the moonlight. Angel didn't begin to describe her.

She shimmied out of the skimpy shorts and settled astride him, her bare thighs contrasting with the dark gray of his slacks. Her hair framed her face in a golden halo, her pink-tipped breasts rose and fell with her breaths. Her waist nipped in, impossibly tiny, and her hips flared out, thighs surrounding his hips.

Striker wrapped his hands around her waist, absorbing the feel of her warm, silky skin. "Okay, now this *is* turning into one of those fantasies."

"Good." She leaned down to kiss him. "Julie told me I should try seducing you."

"She did? When?"

"Last night." Erin rubbed her cheek against his. "We sat up late drinking brandy and cussing you out for walking away from me."

"I'm sorry."

She shrugged. "I can honestly say, I'm over it."

Striker smiled. "I can't believe I ever said no to you."

"Neither can I, quite frankly."

He laughed. "Just for the record, I'm not saying no now."

She pulled back to eye him up and down. "First the seafood fork, and now this? You learn fast."

"I do try."

She sat up straight and stretched her arms over her head, lifting the back of her moonlit hair, trailing it through her fingers. Her nipples hardened in the cold and Striker's body went to full arousal.

"The wind is very sexy, don't you think?" she purred.

He wanted her.

Fast.

Hard.

Here.

Now.

He gripped the lounger arms, reminding himself of his vow to take it slow, hoping for the strength to hold back. "I'm all for sexy," he said, voice strained.

She smiled, running a fingertip in a figure eight pattern over the front of his dress shirt. "You know, I've never made love outside."

"You haven't?"

She shook her head, blinking her deep brown eyes. "You want to be my first?"

Striker clenched his jaw, hard. If she kept this up, her first time outside was going to be over in the blink of an eye.

She reached for his belt, flipping open the clasp, popping the button beneath.

He grabbed her wrist. Willpower was only going to take him so far.

"Problem?" she asked.

He shook his head, trying to sit up and get things back under control. The lightning round earlier on the bathroom sink notwithstanding, women didn't take care of Striker. Striker took care of women.

She placed her hand firmly on his shoulder and pushed him back. "My turn," she said, her voice sultry in the darkness.

"What's turns got to do with anything?"

With her free hand, she reached for his grip on her wrist. "I'm seducing you, remember?"

He knew he shouldn't let her budge that hand. But he gave up his fingers, one at a time, as she slowly, deliberately pried them away from her wrist.

Then she pulled down his zipper, knuckles grazing the front of his boxers. He gasped out loud. This was crazy.

She loosened his pants and took him into her hand. His entire blood supply crested in a rush.

Before he could react, or even get his brain to acknowledge he was in big, big trouble, she straddled him, taking him inside her, surrounding him with tight, fiery heat.

His body jerked against her. "Are you—"

"How's the fantasy going so far, flyboy?" she asked, rocking against him once and nearly sending him to the moon.

He grasped her hips, intending to hold her still. No way was this going to happen again.

But she rocked, and he let her. In fact he helped her. He gripped her hips and drew her against him, rocking her back, once more. And once more. And once more again.

This was way too fast.

This was way too one-sided.

But he couldn't stop.

Sweat popped out on his body. Reason ceased and sensation took over as his blood reached the boiling point.

He knew he was being unforgivably selfish, but her sweet little body was taking him places he'd never been before. He strained toward her, starting to lose focus.

She reached back and gripped his thighs, arching toward the sky, calling his name out over and over again.

He lost the battle, and a starburst of color lit up the moon.

ERIN AWOKE TO SILENCE. Without opening her eyes, she knew Striker had left the bed. She'd been subconsciously aware of his broad, warm body all night long, and now there was only empty air.

She opened her eyes and blinked against the bright sunshine. Trying not to feel disappointed, she turned to face his pillow.

Her heart started to pound.

He'd left a single red rose lying across a folded note on his white pillowcase.

She sat up, curling her legs beneath her and tucking her hair behind her ears. She tentatively reached for the note, telling herself she could handle it if he'd left the island.

Last night had seemed so dreamy and magical that for a few hours she'd allowed herself to believe there was more between them than a fling. But in the cold light of day, she realized that thoughts like that were dangerous.

Striker was Striker. She knew his past. She knew his reputation. She couldn't let herself hope for anything more that a weekend romance. He was leaving today and that was that.

She unfolded the thick sheet of paper.

> Erin,
> You looked so peaceful and beautiful, I couldn't bring myself to wake you. But there was something I had to do. Come and see me at 17 Main Street. Hurry. I miss you already.

It was signed with a bold *S* across the bottom.

Part of her wanted to tuck the note against her chest. The other part wished he'd stop acting like he was her boyfriend.

They weren't in a relationship. It was just a weekend. In fact, it would have been much better if the note had said "Thanks for the memories, see you around, babe." This quasi-romantic stuff put her off balance. She was in danger of wishing for things that couldn't be.

She lifted the rose and inhaled before she realized what she was doing. Its scent was sweet, its petals perfect.

She had to admit, the man sure knew how to give a great fling. No wonder he never struck out.

She slipped out of bed, determinedly leaving the rose behind as she padded into the en suite. The entire time she showered, she told herself she didn't have to go see him. Just because he'd asked, didn't mean she had to rush to his side.

She could back off now, keep it cool for the next couple of hours. Show him she was keeping things in perspective. Maybe he wouldn't even come back to the beach house.

Well, she supposed he'd have to pick up his clothes at some point. But that would be quick. Fifteen, twenty minutes, tops. She'd give him a sophisticated goodbye, let him know she'd had fun, and that would be that.

She could do a classy goodbye for fifteen minutes.

ERIN TOLD HERSELF it could easily have been curiosity that brought her to 17 Main Street. It didn't mean she was pathetically trying to take advantage of every last second with Striker.

And she *was* definitely curious as she wandered up the driveway of the private home. She wondered who Striker could possibly be visiting on Blue Earth Island. As she grew close to the house, she heard voices from the open garage door.

She altered her course, peering in at a bright red-and-silver airplane.

Striker was at a workbench, his muscles flexing beneath his T-shirt as he turned something big made of metal. Her heart fluttered at the sight, and she had to admit she was developing a weakness for a hard-working man.

He caught a glimpse of her, did a double take, and his eyes lit up as though she had just made his day. He abandoned the workbench to head toward her.

"Hey, sweetheart." He dropped a slow kiss on her mouth. "I've been waiting for you."

As she blinked into his warm, welcoming blue eyes, she realized she'd made a big mistake in coming here. The man had charm down to an art form. If she wasn't careful, she'd get swept right up in the fantasy.

"Sleep well?" he asked, brushing a strand of hair from her forehead.

She nodded, steeling herself against his touch. It was like he said, he was an uncouth bohemian with charm. This was all part of his practiced hound-dog routine, and she wasn't the first or last woman who would melt from it.

While she tried to get her heart rate back to normal, he gestured to the plane, grinning like a twelve-year-old.

"Look what I bought," he said.

For a second there, she thought he meant the plane. She glanced around at the tools and airplane parts scattered around the garage. "What?"

He pointed straight at the plane. "Well, half of it anyway."

Erin glanced up at his beaming expression. "What are you talking about?"

He just smiled wider.

She couldn't believe it. "You bought half a plane?"

"That's right."

"But…" What was he thinking? How could he afford it?

An older man appeared through the side door. "Molly's already spending the money," he chuckled at Striker. "She's on the phone right now, making plans to go visit Ben."

He stopped talking when he saw Erin.

"Roger," said Striker. "This is my friend, Erin." He gave her a significant squeeze around the shoulders. A squeeze that told Roger they were more than just friends.

Unfortunately, it also managed to convince a small part of Erin they were more than just friends. She had to stop letting herself react to his meaningless words and gestures.

"Hello, Erin," said Roger, coming forward to shake her hand.

"Nice to meet you," she said automatically, still recovering from Striker's intimate squeeze, and scrambling with the fact that he had bought a plane—on impulse, apparently.

It was a little, old plane, sure. But it still had to cost thousands of dollars.

She went up on her toes and leaned close to his ear. "How can you afford this?"

"I have a good credit rating," he whispered back.

"Are you sure this is such a good idea?"

"Don't worry about it."

"Striker…"

"Erin. I'm not impoverished."

Well, maybe not. But there was a lot of real estate between impoverished and impulsive airplane purchases.

Maybe this was why Striker hadn't made it very far in life. Maybe he blew all his money on impulse.

"Sure do appreciate this," said Roger to Striker.

"Not a problem," said Striker. He let go of Erin and headed over to a sink to wash his hands, speaking over his shoulder while he scrubbed. "Like I said, I've got to get back to the mainland," he said to Roger. "But I'll come over again next week. Maybe we can install the engine before summer ends."

"Looking forward to it," said Roger, beaming.

It was obvious that Striker had made the older man very happy. But at what cost?

Striker dried his hands on a paper towel and crossed the garage to Erin, taking her hand. "You want to hang out in town for a while?"

*Tell him you're busy. Tell him you have to get back to the beach house.*

"I thought we could take a walk through the park, maybe stop at a café?"

She tried to shake her head, but somehow she couldn't get it to move. "Uh, sure," she said instead.

"Great." He led her through the open door.

"When do you have to leave?" she asked, hoping it would be soon.

"I figure I've got about three hours. You want to get some lunch? Walk on the beach? Sit in the park and kiss a while?"

Okay. Three hours. She could do three hours. It didn't really matter where they went, as long as she kept her dignity about her and let him know she was sophisticated enough to handle the goodbye.

"What about windsurfing?" he asked.

"Windsurfing?"

He pointed to the beach. "Ever tried it? We can rent them. It's a perfect day."

She stared at the colorful sails flapping atop wobbly surfboards with figures clinging precariously to crossbars as they careened through the waves. "I don't think…"

"You'll love it."

"Are you trying to kill me?" Now that would be a neat end to their relationship. No uncomfortable letters or phone calls. Nothing to remind him that he'd met and slept with a girl in Pelican Cove. Not that she had any intention of contacting him after this weekend.

He tugged her across the street towards a beach access path. "Of course I'm not trying to kill you. I'm trying to help you have fun."

She wasn't touching that one. "I don't have a bathing suit," she said.

"You can go in your shorts. Come on. Live a little. You know, Julie thinks you work too hard."

"Who says?"

"Julie says."

"You're making that up."

He shook his head. "Nope."

The paved path gave way to fine, white sand. It packed into Erin's sandals as she took the first few steps. "Well Julie doesn't know what she's talking about."

"Sure she does." He gave her a cajoling smile. "Come windsurfing with me. It'll make a new woman out of you."

"What's wrong with the old woman?"

Striker suddenly stopped, pivoting around to face her. His eyes darkened and she got a funny hollow feeling in her stomach. Oh, boy.

He rubbed his hands up and down her bare arms. "Absolutely nothing."

He wasn't serious, she reminded herself. He said these kinds of things to women all the time. If she valued her sanity, she'd simply ignore him.

But he smiled again, and her heart fluttered, and her soul felt as though it was melting for him.

Oh, boy. Crashing through the waves at a hundred miles an hour was probably one of the smarter ways to spend the rest of the morning.

At least then Striker wouldn't be staring at her. Or touching her. Or saying things that made her swoon.

Now that she thought about it, windsurfing looked perfectly safe.

# 11

STRIKER HAD HAD a blast teaching Erin to windsurf. She was awkward at first, spending way more time in the water than on the board. But her sense of humor and an unexpected zest for adventure saw her through. By the end of the two-hour rental, she was zipping along the surf like a pro.

Striker had enjoyed every minute right along with her. It didn't hurt that he needed to get up close and personal helping her on the board. He loved touching her, loved laughing with her, loved the way she looked in her wet shorts and T-shirt.

As they headed through the front door of the beach house, damp and tired, he found himself wondering if he could get away with spending another night on the island. She was planning to present Allan with the offer tonight and fly back to New York tomorrow.

If he blew off the Reeves-DuCarter shareholders meeting, he could spend another evening with her, not to mention another night. Maybe he could help her with the offer to Allan. He had to admit, he was curious to find out if she'd succeed.

He truly wanted her to succeed.

He shut the door behind them, gazing at her wet hair plastered against her head, her glowing cheeks and her long, soft lashes. The drowned rat look worked on her.

"Think you might try it again someday?" he asked.

"Maybe after I recover," she laughed. "I can hardly move my arms."

He leaned forward and grasped her elbow, moving her forearm up and down. "Better think about some weight training to go with the butt master."

"Hey, I'm—"

Julie appeared at the top of the stairs.

Striker let go of Erin's arm and took a step away. "Hi, Julie."

"Where'd you take off to this morning?" asked Erin, smoothing back her damp hair.

Julie didn't answer, but her gaze darted to the bottom of the stairs. Striker followed it. One of her suitcases was packed and waiting.

As she came around the end of the railing, he realized she was carrying her other bag.

Erin started toward her. "What on earth—"

Julie lifted her chin and tossed her hair back as he walked purposefully down the stairs. "I was thinking maybe I'd just take off."

"Take off?" Erin asked blankly, blinking.

Striker wondered if they'd somehow offended her by leaving her alone for the entire morning.

Julie got to the bottom of the stairs and gave a shrug. "Yeah. You know, all you have left to do is present the contract. You don't really need me anymore."

Erin took a couple more steps toward her, eyes narrowing. "Why would you leave early? I thought you were having a great time?"

Striker had to admit, he'd thought the same thing. He also had to admit the thought of having Erin all to himself was very appealing. Not that he wanted Julie to cut her vacation short.

Still, if it was just Erin tonight…

"I'm a little bored," said Julie.

Erin's voice rose an octave. "Bored? You're living an all-expense-paid lifestyle, working on your tan, hanging out with a diamond mine owner who's showing you rare emeralds. How on earth can you be bored?"

"It's not all it's cracked up to be."

"What's not all it's cracked up to be?"

Instead of answering, Julie turned to Striker. "Can I catch a ride with you today?"

Striker hesitated. He wasn't ready to commit to going back to Seattle this afternoon. Though, if necessary, he supposed he could drop Julie and then return to the island.

"Julie, *what* is going on?" asked Erin, moving directly in front of her friend.

"Nothing," said Julie with a little shake of her head, but she didn't look Erin in the eye.

"Will you quit lying," said Erin. "You're really not all that good at it."

Julie met Erin's gaze. "Yes, I am."

"No, you're not. We just humor you." Erin smiled, in an obvious attempt to break the tension.

Julie's expression didn't change.

Erin sobered, her eyes suddenly going wide, voice changing to a worried rush. "Did you have a fight with Allan?"

Julie flinched. "No."

Erin touched Julie's shoulder. "Yes, you did. Tell me what happened."

"We didn't fight, okay?"

"Then, what…" She stared intently at her friend. "Oh, my God. *Julie.*"

Striker glanced from woman to woman, wondering what the heck he'd just missed.

"It's nothing," said Julie, looking away.

"I can't believe it," said Erin.

Julie's lips thinned and she put her hands on her hips, shifting out to one side. "Okay. So I can't sleep with a man and lie to him at the same time. Surprise, even Julie has her standards."

Striker straightened in shock.

Allan had slept with Julie?

He'd *slept* with her.

Why would he sleep with her?

"Of course I'm not surprised you have standards," said Erin evenly. "And you're *not* lying to him."

Striker opened his mouth to ask Julie for clarification, but she cut him off with another question to Erin.

"What would you call it then?"

Erin hesitated. "Okay, so *I'm* lying to him."

Julie bent down to pick up the second suitcase and Striker quickly stepped forward to help her. He took them both from her hands.

"I gotta go," she said.

Erin held up a hand to stop her. "Wait a minute. If there's something happening between the two—"

"Damn it," Julie grimaced. "Nothing's going to happen between us. He's a rich, successful guy and I'm a con artist."

Striker clamped his jaw, struggling with what to keep quiet and what to give up. Allan already knew about the contract. He'd turned the tables on them. And Striker was a party to it.

Erin jumped in. "You're not—"

"I feel like crap," said Julie. "I don't want to face him. Okay?"

Erin's voice went soft. "Maybe he'll understand."

Julie shook her head. "He's not going to understand."

"I can talk to him," said Erin. "I'll explain that you had nothing to do with—"

"No. Don't change the game plan. There's too much at stake for you. I'm fine." She scrubbed a hand across her cheek. "Striker, just… I gotta… " She shook her head. "Excuse me." She turned and trotted up the stairs.

"I'll talk to him," Erin called after her.

"Don't," Julie called back.

"Maybe he'll—"

"Don't," Julie repeated firmly, disappearing into her room.

A sinking feeling slid through Striker's stomach as he set the suitcases down. He had to tell Erin the truth. But what truth, and how much?

"This is a disaster," she said, shoulders slumping. "My boss was so sure it would work. But every time I turn around it gets *more* complicated."

She didn't know the half of it. Striker was about to make it even more complicated.

He cringed. "Uh, Erin?"

"What?" she sighed.

He took a bracing breath, his chest tightening, his stomach clamping. She was not going to be happy about this.

"Allan knows," he said.

"Allan knows what?"

"He knows you and Julie are after a contract."

Erin froze. Her jaw went lax. "You *told* him?"

"No, I didn't *tell* him. As soon as he found out you were from Elle Jewelers, he put two and two together."

She took a pace toward Striker, peering intently into his eyes. "You *knew* he knew?"

He shifted his glance. "Yeah."

"And you didn't *tell* us?"

"I didn't think it was my place."

"Not your place? You're a member of the team. We're *paying* you."

He was also Allan's friend. And his own ethics with Erin were on shaky ground. "I quit, remember?"

"Oh, and that makes everything okay? Why would he take advantage of her? Was it some sick form of revenge?"

"Of course not. Allan's—"

"I can't believe you let him do it."

"I didn't exactly let him…"

Erin's eyes took on a purposeful glare that made Striker nervous. "Well, I don't care *who* he is." She squared her shoulders and marched for the front door. "He's messed with the wrong women this time. I'm not going to let him go around—"

Striker realized with a sudden horror that she was going to confront Allan. "Erin, you can't—"

"Can't what?" She turned. "Can't defend my friend? Can't hold Allan accountable?"

"You can't throw away your career like this. Walk away from the contract if you have to, but—"

"And let him get *away* with it?"

"You're not thinking clearly."

"*Clearly?*" She folded her arms across her chest. "This is the clearest I've been thinking in days."

"Erin, please—"

"Patrick was wrong. Business is business and

friendship is friendship. I don't know why I ever thought I could blur the lines."

"Wait a few minutes, at least until you calm down."

"I *am* calm."

If this was calm, Striker sure didn't want to experience upset. "Let me talk to him," he said.

"And say what, hound-dog Striker? You mean to tell me *you're* going to take the moral high ground?"

"Are *you*?"

Hurt flashed through her eyes, and Striker immediately cringed. He hadn't meant that the way it sounded. "Erin, I'm—"

"Forget it."

He shot for the door to cut her off. As a last resort, he'd physically stop her from confronting Allan until she calmed down. "You want me to beat him up for you?" he joked.

Erin shook her head, reaching for the doorknob. "I don't need your help. It's my company, my deal, my mistake."

"So *you're* going to beat him up?"

She didn't smile.

He sidled a little closer, lowering his voice. "Erin, you have to be professional about this."

She blinked up at him, determination shining from her eyes. "Professional is what I should have been all along. I let my boss convince me schmoozing was okay. He was wrong, and I was wrong to believe him."

There was a passion behind her words that Striker couldn't help but admire. She was misguided, and she'd understand that eventually, but he couldn't help but respect her determination to stick to her principles. He should take a lesson.

He put his hand over hers, preventing her from opening the door. "Stop and think about this before you do irreparable damage."

"Haven't you heard a word I said?"

There was a sharp knock from the other side of the door.

ERIN JUMPED BACK in shock.

But when she peered through the opaque window and saw that it was Allan on the front porch, her momentary shock turned to anger. She reached for the knob, but Striker stopped her.

"Erin." His tone was a warning growl next to her ear.

"Let go of me," she said.

"No."

"I don't want to pull rank."

"You can't pull rank. I quit yesterday."

Allan knocked again, harder this time.

"He can see us through the window," she pointed out.

"I'm not letting you do this."

His attempt to save her was sweet, but misdirected.

She composed herself and stared directly into his eyes. "I'm calm. I'm reasonable. I'm fine."

His brows knit together. "You sure?"

"I'm sure. Now please let go of my hand."

He slowly, hesitantly withdrew.

Finally.

She swung open the door and glared at Allan. "I don't know who the hell you think you are."

"Erin!"

Her voice vibrated. "But nobody treats Julie like that and gets away with it."

Allan blinked, looking stunned.

Striker jumped in. "Allan, they're—"

"Stay out of this," she hissed at Striker, locking eyes with Allan. "Just because you have money and power and influence, doesn't mean you can treat women—"

"Where's Julie?" asked Allan.

Erin folded her arms across her wet shirt. "Nowhere that you're ever going to see her again."

"I need to see her," said Allan, shifting forward.

"I don't think so," said Erin.

Allan looked as though he might bodily move Erin out of the way.

"You'll still have to go through me." Striker's voice was deep and sure behind her.

Allan's gaze shifted to Striker's and locked. After a few seconds he faded back. "Is Julie upset?"

Erin let out a laugh of disbelief. "Why would she be upset? Just because you thought sex was part of the business deal."

Allan blinked. "Business deal?"

"Don't play dumb with me," said Erin. "*I* know *you* know." She poked his chest with her index finger. "She was here as a gemologist, not a—"

Striker grabbed her wrist and pulled it away from Allan's chest.

She shot him a glare of disbelief. Here she thought he'd switched to *her* team.

"Julie told you that?" asked Allan. "She actually *told* you I coerced her?"

"Ye—" Erin paused. She flipped through the conversation with Julie.

Well, no. Not exactly. Julie had said she felt guilty and wanted to leave the island…

Allan turned his attention to Striker. "I *am* going to see Julie."

Erin frantically tried to piece things together.

"She's pretty upset," said Striker.

"Well, I don't know why she would be," said Allan, confusion growing on his face. "We just… It was… Oh, for the love of God, let me talk to her."

"What are you going to say?" asked Striker.

Julie had felt guilty.

Striker had said Allan knew about the contract.

"What I want to say to her is personal," said Allan. "It won't upset her."

Erin had assumed that Allan somehow extorted sex. Which was a reasonable assumption given that he had to know how much Julie wanted his contract.

"Convince me," said Striker to Allan.

Except that he never told Julie he knew about the contract. Which meant he couldn't have bribed her.

Which put a huge flaw in Erin's theory.

"Do we *really* have to do this?" asked Allan.

Which meant Erin might have just insulted the biggest potential client Elle Jewelers had ever had.

"You can talk to her," said Striker. "But I don't leave the room."

Erin's stomach clenched around nothing. She'd insulted him for no good reason.

Allan shook his head. "Your choice." He brushed his way past Striker. "But you're going to feel really stupid."

As Allan headed for the staircase, Erin put a hand on Striker's arm, squeezing tight. "Uh, Striker?"

"Yeah?"

"Did you think Allan coerced Julie into having sex with him?"

"I don't want to believe it…"

Allan took the stairs two at a time.

"He didn't tell her he knew about the contract," said Erin, looking up at Striker. "How did he coerce her if he didn't tell her about the contract?"

Julie's bedroom door opened and they both turned their attention to the top of the stairs.

Allan spoke to Julie for a few seconds, his low words muffled by the distance. Then he pulled something out of his pocket and dropped down on one knee.

Erin's heart sank. This didn't look much like co-ercion. She had a horrible feeling her career had just ended for no reason.

Allan opened the velvet box and Julie's eyes went wide as saucers as he slid a ring on her finger. She dropped to her knees and wrapped her arms around his neck.

Allan grinned like a maniac and held her close.

"Allan was right," said Striker into Erin's ear. "I do feel really stupid."

Julie said something to Allan and he laughed. Standing, he took her hand and pulled her to her feet.

"Erin!" she called down the stairs, waving her fingers. "It's an ideal-cut, two-carat, blue-white flawless. With an emerald. I think he really loves me."

Erin couldn't help smiling.

So her career had tanked? So she'd insulted her best friend's fiancé?

At least Julie was happy.

Allan took her hand as they came down the stairs and she rushed over to show Erin the ring, tears glistening in her eyes. The stones were stunning and the setting was perfect. A knotted gold band, with smooth swirls holding the big stones.

Erin hugged Julie. There was no way to be anything but thrilled.

"So, let's take a look at that contract," said Allan.

Erin drew back from Julie, her jaw dropping open. "But…"

Striker pressed his elbow against her ribs. "Get the nice man the contract, sweetheart."

Erin didn't understand. "But I accused you of coercing sex from Julie."

Striker pressed harder. "*Erin*," he muttered under his breath.

"I know," said Allan, slipping an arm around Julie's shoulders. "You're quite the little pit bull when you're upset."

Erin didn't know how to respond to that.

"You're exactly the kind of person I want on my team. So, make me an offer. Let's get this negotiation over with so we can go celebrate."

# 12

THE WAVES LAPPED against Striker's feet as he and Erin walked hand in hand along the beach. The sun was just starting to set, and they'd left Allan and Julie sharing a bottle of champagne on the deck of a local restaurant.

Allan had signed the contract and everyone seemed to be floating on air. Everyone except Striker.

Watching Allan and Julie together made him feel empty. He'd thought sleeping with Erin would be enough. With her, he'd already broken his all-time record for staying with a woman. Which, sadly, wasn't saying much.

He wanted intimacy, he realized, companionship, warm nights by the fire and long conversations over dinner. He wanted somebody to laugh with, somebody who got his jokes, somebody who held him accountable. Somebody with ethics and standards, and the fire inside her to see them through.

He wanted a girlfriend all right. But not just any girlfriend.

He stopped, turning her toward him, taking both her hands in his.

The wind whipped her hair around her face.

He took a deep breath. "What about us?" he asked softly as the waves churned the sand beneath their feet.

"What about us?" she asked in return.

He nodded to where Allan and Julie were still visible on the deck. "You think we can have a happily ever after?"

The expression on her face went slack and her hands trembled slightly beneath his. "What?"

"You and me. You think we can do something with us?"

Her eyes dimmed and Striker's stomach clenched.

She shook her head. "We had a good time, Striker. But it's time to stop the fantasy."

"But—"

"We're from different worlds," she said. "I knew that going in."

Striker wasn't ready to give up that easily. "Allan and Julie were from different worlds, too."

Erin withdrew her hands. "That's different."

"How is it different?"

"Julie *wants* to live in Allan's world."

Striker took a small step back, the cold ocean creeping up his calf. "But you don't want to live in my world, is that it?"

"Don't do this," she whispered. "I can't—"

"Don't do what? Invite you to see where this is going? Invite you to share my life?"

"Even if you were…"

"Even if I were what?"

She laughed, sounding jaded and worldly wise. "I live in Manhattan. You fix old airplanes in Seattle. What would we do? How would it work? Exactly how much do you want from me?"

So, that was it. In her eyes, he was still the uncouth charter pilot. He was beneath her stature, not welcome in her world.

Something flickered then died inside of Striker. "I guess I want to be the guy who's important enough for you to change worlds."

"Striker." Her tone was pleading.

He shook his head. He could tell her he was rich and then maybe she'd say yes. He could tell her that his world and her world weren't so far apart.

But he wouldn't.

He reached out and touched her cheek one last time.

Striker the charter pilot *was* Striker the millionaire. But she couldn't have one without the other.

"Goodbye, Erin."

Her lower lip trembled. For a second there, he thought she might kiss him.

But she didn't.

She took another step away, and the moment passed.

Striker had just struck out.

ERIN STARED AT the sunrise from her new ninth-floor office at Elle's headquarters wondering for the thousandth time if Striker might have been serious. Then, for the thousandth time, she dismissed it as ridiculous.

He was now and always had been a hound dog. He'd been giving her a good fling, that was all. The sweet words, the romantic note, the rose, the tender declaration that he wanted to pursue a relationship, it was all part of his routine.

If she'd said yes, he might have spent another night with her, maybe another day, then he would have rode off into the sunset with sweet promises to call her.

But he never would.

This way, her heartache was over with quickly and cleanly. Another week, two at the most, and he'd be a footnote. She'd definitely made the right decision.

The right decision.

It had been three sleepless nights since she'd made the right decision. Three sleepless nights and two frantic days of board meetings and congratulatory calls. She was the new golden child of Elle and everybody wanted her time.

Patrick sauntered in through her open office door. "How's my favorite buyer today?"

She mustered up a smile. She had to stop wondering what Striker was doing. Probably with another woman already, that's what.

"I'm a little tired," she said to Patrick.

"Get used to it. They want you to fly to Burma next week."

Burma? Her?

"Rubies?" she asked.

"You got it. Charles was slated to make the trip, but they need him in Russia, and you're next on the list. Since Julie's not available, they want you to take Scott." Patrick turned his thumb and index finger into a mock gun and pretended to shoot her as he walked out of the office. "First class all the way from here on in."

Flying to Burma for rubies. It was a dream come true. And Scott was one of the best—a gifted gemologist, attractive, intelligent, loaded with class.

So why did she suddenly picture a sweaty, dusty Striker working on a little plane six hours in the opposite direction of Burma?

She scrunched her eyes shut. What if he'd been serious?

No, no, no. She wasn't going to think that way. He wasn't serious. And even if he was, what was she supposed to do? Give up everything she'd ever worked for and go live above an airplane garage on the West Coast?

What if he spent all their money buying decrepit old planes? What if they had children and had to raise them in a stuffy little one bedroom garage apartment, never having new clothes, always longing for the toys they could only see on TV?

Besides, he wasn't serious.

If she went back to Blue Earth Island, she'd only make a fool of herself.

She clicked on her computer, bringing up a report that was due in two days. The words and figures blurred in front of her eyes.

She clamped a hand over her forehead.

If she didn't go back, she'd never know.

Was it worth her pride and her future to find out if he'd been serious?

"Erin?" Her secretary stuck her head through the doorway. "Should I book the Burma tickets for tomorrow?"

Erin stared at her secretary in silence, her fingers tightening around her pen. *Was* he the guy worth changing worlds for?

"Erin?"

Her heart rate sped up and she could feel perspiration break out all over her body.

"Give me a couple of days," she said. "There's something I have to do."

DEREK'S FOOTFALLS ECHOED on the wooden steps as he sauntered up to Striker's deck overlooking the rocky shore of Puget Sound.

"Mom was disappointed when you didn't make the shareholders meeting," he said.

Striker took a sip of his beer. "I got held up."

Taking the deck chair next to Striker, Derek mimicked his posture, putting his feet up on the low rail and scooping a can of beer out of the ice chest between the chairs.

"Women'll do that to you," he said, popping the tab.

"Who says it was a woman? I was out flying."

Derek took a drink. "Uh-huh. Bet her name was Erin."

"Erin went back to New York."

"Alone?"

Striker shrugged. "How would I know?"

Derek grinned. "You leave her or she leave you?"

Striker didn't answer.

"Finally struck out, did you?"

Striker shot his brother a glare.

Derek just kept grinning. "Just between us, what did you do to piss her off?"

Striker stared at a pair of gulls swooping over the waves in the bright sunlight. He took a swig of his beer. What the hell? "I asked her to stay."

Derek nodded sagely. "Ouch."

"You're telling me."

"She wasn't interested?"

Striker shrugged. "She told me I didn't fit her world."

"What world is that? Monogamy?"

Striker clenched his fist. He'd never, not in a million years, *ever* screw around on Erin. "Give me a break."

"You're in love with her."

Striker closed his eyes. It just plain ripped his guts out to hear someone say it out loud.

Derek's tone turned serious. "What world didn't you fit, Striker?"

"She thinks I'm an uncouth, bohemian, floatplane pilot who doesn't have two nickels to rub together."

Derek was silent for a moment. "Well, since you and I both know that's not true, where the hell did she get that idea?"

"I was working on the Cessna when she met me."

"And?"

"I thought she was a bit of a snob, so I never bothered to correct her initial assumption."

"Even when you fell in love with her?"

"I didn't…" Striker shifted his feet from the railing. "That was later."

"Let me get this straight. You asked her to marry you, but she—"

"I didn't ask her to marry me."

Derek paused. "What did you ask her?"

"I asked her to hang around so we could see where the relationship went."

Derek nodded. "Oh, well, what woman wouldn't swoon at an offer like that? Did you mention you owned a house or did she think she'd have to bunk out in your plane?"

"Did you just drop by to ride my ass?"

"Well, somebody's got to do it. You love her, Striker. You, *you* are ready to pledge monogamy to her, but you didn't bother to tell her you could keep food on the table?"

"I wanted her to stay for me."

"What else would she stay for?"

"My money."

"She didn't know about your money."

Striker felt vindicated. "And she didn't stay, did she?"

Derek sighed and sat back in his chair. "Do you love her?"

Striker sighed. "That's irrelevant."

Derek spoke slowly. "Do you love her?"

"Yes," Striker hissed. He loved Erin. He was madly, passionately in love with Erin. He couldn't think of any greater heaven than spending his life with her. And he couldn't think of any worse hell than spending it without her.

Derek drained his beer and plunked the can down on the wood floor of the deck. "Then you use everything you have to win her."

"Including the money?"

"Especially the money."

"Why?"

"Because that's how it works," said Derek.

"That's ridiculous."

"She ever been without money?"

Striker paused. "She grew up poor. She hated it."

"And you asked her to dive right back into that lifestyle." Derek chuckled darkly. "You don't win a woman by looking as unappealing as possible, Striker. Jeez, you can be stupid sometimes."

Derek wasn't exactly the oracle of wisdom, but his words gave Striker pause.

"You win her by making yourself look good," said Derek.

Striker hated to admit it, but his brother was right. He'd asked Erin to give up everything *but* him. He'd given her an impossible choice, and then asked her to make it. Change worlds for him?

What the hell had he been thinking?

STRIKER STOOD IN FRONT of his father's desk, looking Jackson directly in the eye. "I've been doing a lot of thinking the last few days."

Jackson nodded, barely glancing up from the report in front of him. "Well, I suppose you had to do something while you weren't flying."

He flipped to the last page and began scrolling his signature. "I hope you're not here to try to convince me to let you go back up in the jet."

Striker tried not to grin. "No. I'm here to tell you that you were right."

Jackson stopped writing. He peered up at Striker. "About what?"

"About me."

Jackson's eyes narrowed. "In what way?"

Striker should have known his father wouldn't make this easy. If capitulation was what it took, fine. "I've been cavalier and irresponsible."

"I thought you said you weren't here to convince me to put you back in the jet."

"I'm not."

Jackson gestured with his pen. "Then what the hell was that all about?"

"I was serious."

"Striker, my son, you are the master of saying things that people want to hear. You do it with women. You do it with your mother. And you try to do it with me."

"But—"

"I can't bring myself to believe that you took off for four days, had an epiphany, and are ready to repent and change your life."

Striker clenched his jaw. He was capitulating here. He was giving his father everything his own way. Why did Jackson *still* have to argue?

The urge to walk out of the room was strong. But he fought it. "I'm serious," he repeated. "No more joyrides, no more pickups, no more goofing off while I'm on duty."

"What's the catch?"

Striker shook his head. "No catch."

Jackson's eyebrows arched.

"Well, there is one little favor I need before I turn into a flawless son."

"And that is?"

"I need to borrow the jet to impress a woman."

Jackson's jaw dropped open.

"You'll like her, I promise." Striker grinned.

"I don't believe—"

"Dad." Striker smiled. "I can see your grandchildren in her eyes."

Jackson froze. The chill went out of his eyes. "*That* kind of woman?"

Striker nodded. "That kind of woman. Her name's Erin, and she's in New York, and I've got some serious explaining to do."

"And you need my jet to do it with."

"Pretty much."

"You promise you'll bring her home to meet your mother."

"Tomorrow."

Jackson smiled and dropped his pen onto the desktop.

ERIN RUSHED DOWN the causeway at Sea Tac Airport, her cell phone to her ear. She was trying frantically to line up a flight from the Seattle Harbor to Blue Earth Island. She'd left New York in such a hurry this morning that she didn't have time to finalize plans.

The charter company had one of those annoying answering systems that made a person press a thousand buttons to get a recorded voice mail telling them to call back later.

She snapped the phone shut and stuffed it back into her purse. She'd try again from the taxi. Hiking her carry-on bag up farther on her shoulder, she glanced around to get her bearings.

She thought the exit was in front of her, but maybe...

Through the glass wall, to the unsecured side of

the terminal, she saw a man walk by and did a double take. Her chest contracted.

Striker?

Here.

In Seattle.

She rushed backward, coming up to the glass, banging on it with the flat of her hand. Several people turned to stare, but she ignored them. She banged again.

He turned.

Finally.

His eyes widened, his mouth curved into a welcoming smile. She knew with an instantaneous certainty that he was glad to see her. It wasn't just an act.

Maybe none of it had been an act.

He moved to the window, put his hand up against hers, then pointed the direction she should go. She nodded, walking next to him down the concourse, grinning like an idiot.

When she came to a solid wall and he disappeared from view, she picked up her pace. Then she started to jog, dragging her wheeled suitcase behind her, struggling to keep her purse and carry-on secured on her shoulder.

She rushed through the security door and came face to face with him.

He pulled her into his arms, lifting her, bags and all, off the floor. "What are you *doing?*" he asked, his cheek pressed to hers, his voice rumbling in her ear.

She closed her eyes and absorbed his touch. Contentment settled deep into her soul. She'd made it. New York, Seattle or Blue Earth Island, wherever Striker was, was home.

They'd get by somehow. Elle had retail stores on the West Coast, surely they'd be interested in someone with her experience.

"Erin?" he prompted, reminding her that he'd asked a question.

"I came back," she said.

He drew back to gaze at her. "What for?"

She experienced a fleeting moment of doubt. "Were you serious?"

"About what?"

"About wanting me to stay?"

"Oh, yeah. I was—"

"Then I'll stay. I don't know what I'll do. I don't know what we'll do. I mean, I hope you don't want to buy too many planes, because—"

"Erin?"

"Yeah?"

"Before we have this conversation, can I show you something?"

"Sure." She glanced around. "So, what are *you* doing here?"

He lifted the bag off her shoulder and settled it on his own. Then he took the handle of her suitcase. "Traveling pretty light for somebody who came back forever."

She bit her bottom lip. "I wasn't sure—"

His midnight-blue eyes caught hers and he took her hand. "*I'm* sure." He kissed her knuckles, glancing around the crowded terminal. "This is probably the worst place in the world to say this, but I love you, Erin."

Happiness engulfed Erin's entire body. "I love you too, Striker."

He gave her a quick kiss. "Isn't this going to make an interesting story to tell our grandchildren?"

"Grandchildren?"

He started walking, guiding her with him through the crowd. "I was kind of hoping you wanted kids."

"Well, uh, sure."

"Since I promised my parents we would."

"You told your parents about me?"

"They can't wait to meet you." He zipped a card into a card lock and a door buzzed open. "They're going to love you."

Erin glanced around. "Striker, where are we—"

"It's okay. I'm a pilot."

They started down a long hallway. "I know you're a pilot, but—"

"Hey, Striker." A security guard nodded.

"Hi, Bert."

Erin craned her neck to look at the man as they hurried past. "You *know* him?"

"Yeah."

"I thought you flew a floatplane."

"I fly lots of things."

They made their way down a staircase, under a canopy and out onto the tarmac.

Striker gestured to a gleaming white jet. "What do you think?"

Erin looked around. "What?"

"It's mine."

Erin stopped dead still. "*What?*"

"Well, ten percent of it."

She opened her mouth. Nothing but a rasping sound came out. She swallowed. "You bought…" He couldn't have bought a jet. He was joking.

They were never going to be able to afford food.

Striker stopped beside her. "Well, actually, it's owned by Reeves-DuCarter International."

Okay, that made more sense.

"I own ten percent of Reeves-DuCarter."

Erin stared up at him. "*The* Reeves-DuCarter."

He nodded. "I—"

"*The Reeves-DuCarter,*" she repeated on a squeak.

"I was on my way to New York," he said softly. "To apologize and tell you we can live any damn lifestyle you want."

She blinked. Then she blinked again. "Are you telling me you're a rich man?"

He looked away. "Eight figures, just like Allan."

Erin's knees went weak. Good God, she'd tried to give the man fashion advice. She'd told him which fork to use. She'd cut his hair.

"Erin?"

"Why?"

He gave her a sheepish grin. "See, I didn't actually ever tell you I was only a floatplane pilot, you just assumed I had no class."

She bopped him in the arm. "You tried to buy the ugliest suit I have ever seen."

"Okay, so maybe I hammed it up a little."

"A *little?*"

"You were so damn fun to tease."

She stared at him. "How well do you know Allan?"

Striker shrugged. "Pretty well."

"You *did* tell him we were after a contract."

Striker held up his hands. "No. He figured it out that night at dinner. I never lied to you, Erin. Not about anything. You are the most beautiful woman I've ever laid eyes on, and I love you very much."

The fight left her. "You were coming to New York?"

"I was coming to New York." He gestured to the jet. "But we can go wherever you want."

"Right now?"

"Right now. Only thing is, we'd better stay on this continent. I promised my dad I'd have you and the jet home by tomorrow."

# Epilogue

STRIKER'S YOUNGER BROTHER Tyler whistled low under his breath as he handed Striker a beer on the grassy lawn of his lakefront home. He nodded to Erin who was being warmly welcomed by Striker's mother and his sister-in-law, Jenna. "I can see why you were nearly incoherent."

Striker accepted the beer. "What are you talking about?"

Derek trotted down the steps to join them on the lawn.

"Derek said you could barely get out a proper sentence on the phone."

Derek chuckled.

"Derek's a lunatic," said Striker.

"How'd you get a woman like that to give you the time of day?" asked Tyler.

"Derek's not a lunatic," said Derek. "He's older and wiser than both of you."

"Yeah?" said Striker. "Then how come Derek's the only guy who's stag tonight?"

"Like I said, I'm older and wiser." He tipped up his beer.

Tyler grinned at his oldest brother. "Don't worry, bro. Jenna invited Candice to keep you company."

Derek stared at Tyler. *"What?"*

Tyler nodded.

"It's bad enough that I've got to put up with her all day long, now she's invading my weekends?"

"Jenna thought she could help with the wedding plans."

Derek snorted. "Right. That woman would take a wrecking ball to the church steeple to make it fit in the pictures."

"Who's Candice?" asked Striker, his gaze drifting past Derek's shoulder to watch Erin. She fit. Chatting with his mother, laughing with Jenna. She *so* fit.

"She's our decorator," said Derek.

"I thought Jenna was your decorator."

"It's a sort of Dr. Jekyll and Mr. Hyde partnership," said Derek. "Jenna's the nice decorator. Candice is the evil maniac."

Tyler pointed at Derek around his beer can. "You be nice."

*"Me* be nice?"

Striker took a couple of steps away from his brothers, drifting toward Erin.

"She's too good for you," called Tyler.

Striker grinned over his shoulder and nodded. "I know. Ain't it great?"

He crossed the lawn to where the women were

chatting among Jenna's rose bushes. Another woman had joined them. Striker assumed it was Candice.

"There's Trinity Church," said his mother. "That would hold four hundred."

"Or St. Paul's, if you want to have it on the East Coast," said Candice.

Erin opened her mouth. "I think—"

"I'm worried about a caterer," said Jenna. "September isn't very far away."

Erin tried again. "What if—"

"Too bad the Lighthouse is completely shut down," said Candice.

Jenna turned to Erin, her eyes shining. "My reception at the Quayside was spectacular."

Striker's mother touched Jenna's arm. "Wouldn't it be wonderful to have another one there?"

Striker's heart swelled with pride. Erin was being so patient with them. They'd talked about a simple ceremony, even considered eloping.

He came up behind her, wrapping his arms around her waist, pulling her close.

"Any chance we could talk you into the Quayside, Striker?" asked Jenna. "Erin would love it."

"We were thinking simple," said Striker.

"You can easily go simple at the Quayside," said his mother. "We'll talk to the event planner about something minimalist."

"The ballroom holds five hundred," said Striker.

His mother blinked at him, clearly confused as to his point.

Jenna held up her hands. "I know the perfect bakery."

Striker whispered in Erin's ear, "You okay?"

She nodded.

Jenna's voice grew more excited. "Maybe a champagne icing, no other color, we could work with texture…"

"I can stop them," he offered to Erin under his breath. "I know you want simple."

"Don't." There was a catch in her voice.

Striker gently turned her in his arms. "Hey…"

Her eyes were shimmering.

"Sweetheart? I can stop them right now."

She put a hand on his bicep and shook her head. "It's a family, Striker."

"I know they can be overwhelming."

She shook her head again. "I've never had this before."

He blinked. "You're okay with them taking over your wedding?"

She smiled. "I can get married at the Met with a thirty-foot train and fifty bridesmaids—"

"Don't say that too loud."

Her smile grew. "As long as you're my groom, nothing else matters. Let them plan it all."

"You sure?"

Striker's mother's voice rose above Jenna's. "I

think a full skirt might be too much. What about something off the shoulder?"

"Have I got a designer for you," said Candice.

Erin blinked rapidly. "I'm going to have brothers and sisters."

Striker glanced around at his meddling, strong-minded family. "Better get to know them before you get all starry-eyed about it."

"I'm going to love them all."

"Yeah? Well, you'd better love me the best."

"Always," she sighed.

He leaned down to kiss her.

Jenna touched Erin's arm, and Erin turned away from the second kiss.

"We've got a really interesting off-white theme going here," said Jenna. "How do you feel about lilies?"

"Love them," said Erin.

"Love you," Striker whispered.

* * * * *

*Don't miss Derek's story*
*coming next month*
*in Harlequin Temptation #1010*
**High Stakes**

**HARLEQUIN® *Blaze*™**

When three women go to a lock-and-key
party to meet sexy singles, they never
expect to find their perfect matches....

# #166 HARD TO HANDLE
## by Jamie Denton
### January 2005

# #170 ON THE LOOSE
## by Shannon Hollis
### February 2005

# #174 SLOW RIDE
## by Carrie Alexander
### March 2005

Indulge in these three blazing hot stories today!

# Lock & Key
### Unlock the possibilities...

*On sale at your favorite retail outlet.*

HBLK04

**Coming in February 2005**
**from**

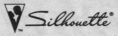

## Margaret Allison's
# A SINGLE DEMAND
### (Silhouette Desire #1637)

Cassie Edwards had gone to a tropical resort
to find corporate raider Steve Axon, but ended up
losing her virginity to a sexy bartender instead.
Cassie then returned home to a surprise:
her bartender *was* Steve Axon! Mixing business
with pleasure was not part of her plan, and
Cassie was determined to forget that night—
but Steve had another demand....

*Available at your favorite retail outlet.*

Visit Silhouette Books at www.eHarlequin.com            SDASD

HARLEQUIN® *Blaze*™

Look for more

*men to do!*

...before you say "I do."
In January 2005 have a taste of

#165 **A LICK AND A PROMISE**
by **Jo Leigh**

Enjoy the latest sexual escapades
in the hottest miniseries

**Only from Blaze**

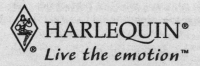

HARLEQUIN®
*Live the emotion*™

**www.eHarlequin.com**                    HBMTD0105

If you enjoyed what you just read,
then we've got an offer you can't resist!

# Take 2 bestselling love stories FREE!

# Plus get a FREE surprise gift!

Clip this page and mail it to Harlequin Reader Service®

**IN U.S.A.**
3010 Walden Ave.
P.O. Box 1867
Buffalo, N.Y. 14240-1867

**IN CANADA**
P.O. Box 609
Fort Erie, Ontario
L2A 5X3

**YES!** Please send me 2 free Harlequin Temptation® novels and my free surprise gift. After receiving them, if I don't wish to receive anymore, I can return the shipping statement marked cancel. If I don't cancel, I will receive 4 brand-new novels each month, before they're available in stores. In the U.S.A., bill me at the bargain price of $3.80 plus 25¢ shipping and handling per book and applicable sales tax, if any*. In Canada, bill me at the bargain price of $4.47 plus 25¢ shipping and handling per book and applicable taxes**. That's the complete price and a savings of 10% off the cover prices—what a great deal! I understand that accepting the 2 free books and gift places me under no obligation ever to buy any books. I can always return a shipment and cancel at any time. Even if I never buy another book from Harlequin, the 2 free books and gift are mine to keep forever.

142 HDN DZ7U
342 HDN DZ7V

| Name | (PLEASE PRINT) | |
|---|---|---|
| Address | Apt.# | |
| City | State/Prov. | Zip/Postal Code |

*Not valid to current Harlequin Temptation® subscribers.*

*Want to try two free books from another series?*
*Call 1-800-873-8635 or visit www.morefreebooks.com.*

\* Terms and prices subject to change without notice. Sales tax applicable in N.Y.
\*\* Canadian residents will be charged applicable provincial taxes and GST.
All orders subject to approval. Offer limited to one per household.
® are registered trademarks owned and used by the trademark owner or its licensee.

TEMP04R                                    ©2004 Harlequin Enterprises Limited

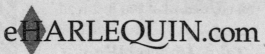

# eHARLEQUIN.com

## The Ultimate Destination for Women's Fiction

Becoming an eHarlequin.com member is easy, fun and **FREE!** Join today to enjoy great benefits:

- **Super savings** on all our books, including members-only discounts and offers!

- Enjoy **exclusive online reads**—FREE!

- Info, tips and **expert advice** on writing your own romance novel.

- FREE romance **newsletters,** customized by you!

- Find out the latest on your **favorite authors.**

- Enter to win exciting **contests and promotions!**

- Chat with other members in our **community message boards!**

**To become a member,**
**visit www.eHarlequin.com today!**

INTMEMB04R